JUST IN TIME FOR LOVE

Other Works by Jan Yager

Novels

The Pretty One

On the Run

Untimely Death (with Fred Yager)

Just Your Everyday People (with Fred Yager)

Dramatic Literature

Please Don't Forget Me: A One-At Play

A Week with Mom: A One-Act Play

Poetry

In Love and Work: Poems

The Healing Power of Creative Mourning: Poems

Children's Books

The Cantaloupe Cat, The Quiet Dog, The Reading Rabbit (Illustrated by Mitzi Lyman)

Fairy Tale Sequels, Book 1 – Little Red Riding Hood

Fairy Tale Sequels, Book 2 – The Three Little Pigs

Fairy Tale Sequels, Book 3 – Goldilocks and the Three Bears

Nonfiction

Time Masters

How to Finish Everything You Start

When Friendship Hurts

The Adjunct's Handbook

Victims

JUST IN TIME FOR LOVE

A Novella

Based on the screenplay, "No Time for Love," by Fred Yager and Jan Yager

JAN YAGER

Hannacroix Creek Books, Inc.
Stamford, CT

For Fred

Published by:
Hannacroix Creek Books, Inc.
1127 High Ridge Road, #110
Stamford, Connecticut 06905 USA

Library of Congress Control Number: 2025927232

ISBN: 978-1-938998-18-8 (trade paperback)
ISBN: 978-1-938998-42-3 (hardcover)
ISBN: 978-1-938998-27-0 (Kindle e-book)

Chapter 1

December dawned, clear and cold, in New York City. The bitter temperatures were offset by the cheerful signs of the upcoming holidays as Park Avenue and other stores along the avenues showcased their best gift ideas amidst sparkling Christmas lights.

This was Kate Hellman's favorite time of winter in Manhattan. She grew up in Center City Philadelphia, but since she had been living in New York City for more than a decade, she considered herself a native New Yorker by now.

December in Manhattan. Everyone seemed friendlier. Even the Santa Clauses on the street corners, ringing their bells as they asked for donations, denoted a holiday spirit that made December somewhat easier for a woman living alone. Her beau of two years, Jennings, was still deciding if he wanted to make a permanent commitment and get married.

But Kate (or Doctor Kate, as some of her students liked to refer to her), was on a crusade to find a husband. It began four weeks previously with a phone call from her older sister, Melanie.

"Hi Kate," Melanie had said. "I've got exciting news!"

"Can't wait to hear it. Did you get a promotion?"

"Much better news than that."

"Do tell!"

"I'm pregnant!"

There was a pause in their conversation. A feeling came over Kate that she'd never felt before. After all, as long as her older sister didn't have a family, Kate felt she had plenty of time to think about such matters. But now, with just two words, Kate's fantasy about how much time she had to start a family of her own was shattered.

Kate had wanted children years before, with her first husband, but when he'd cruelly said, "I'd never want to have children with you," that desire, that longing was put on the back burner. Her post-divorce years, after age twenty-three, were instead filled with school and then building her successful career.

But now, at the relatively old age of thirty-eight in terms of childbearing options, she felt a deep-seated emotion in her gut that could only be called "baby hunger."

After a few deep breaths, and as she held back her tears, Kate finally blurted, "That's great news! I'm so happy for you and Jerry!"

Jerry and Melanie had been married for almost fifteen years. Everyone, including Kate, had given up on them ever having children. She, and her parents, and just about everyone else didn't believe Melanie and Jerry when they said, "We're just waiting till it's the right time." Everyone, including Kate, figured that was just a way to stop nosey relatives, especially their parents, from putting pressure on them.

Alas, with this news, it turned out that they actually meant it.

"It's a girl," Melanie added.

"Oh," said Kate, somewhat sheepishly. "You're far enough along to have had amniocentesis and found out the gender?"

"Yes," Melanie replied. "We're right at sixteen weeks!"

What flashed through Kate's head was how academic and awkward that must have sounded when she said "found out the gender" instead of "found out the sex" like a normal person. Kate instantly reflected on how getting her Ph.D. in sociology just two years before had impacted her view of the world—including her vocabulary.

Sociologists discussed gender and sex as two different concepts. Kate realized that, technically, she should have said "sex" since "gender" refers to the culture associated with being male or female and not the biology.

Melanie, oblivious to her sister's consternation, continued chatting happily.

"Yes, and, fortunately, we also found out the baby's looking normal genetically. We were worried because, as you know, Jerry's mother contracted lupus in her early forties."

"I'm so happy for both of you. I mean, all of us. I'll be your baby's aunt!"

"That's right!"

"Have you chosen a name yet?"

"Jerry and I thought we should take our time in deciding," Melanie replied. "And Carol agreed."

Another emotion overtook Kate. Anger. *My sister's best friend Carol found out about her pregnancy before me*, she thought.

"That's good to know, Melanie. "Thanks so much for sharing the good—no, the great—news, Melanie! I gotta run now."

Kate had to get off the phone. Her emotions were swirling. Jealousy. Anger. Confusion. Not only her wondering where this baby hunger was coming from but the realization that, because of Jennings' ambivalence, she didn't have a fiancé, nor was she living with a romantic partner, let alone a husband. How could she find someone and start a family before her biological clock ran out?

Until that phone call with Melanie, Kate never saw thirty-eight as "old" when it came to her fertility. But now, suddenly, she was wondering just what her statistical chances were to conceive.

She figured this was a question for the #1 search engine that she facetiously referred to as "Doctor Google." "Question: What are a woman's chances of conceiving after the age of thirty-five?"

Answer: "A woman's chances of conceiving begin to decline gradually after age thirty, dropping from about a 20% chance per month in her early thirties to around 15% at age thirty-five, and further to 5% per month by age forty…"

Kate was numb. "After age thirty," she said out loud. She wasn't thinking about babies and marriage at age thirty. A young divorcee, she'd been focused on earning her degree. And at thirty-six, while finishing up her doctorate, she began a committed romantic relationship with Jennings. Throughout her time with Jennings, she assumed they'd eventually get married and start a family. She figured everything would fall into place for her regarding having children.

…That is, before Jennings decided he was commitment phobic as he told Kate that he needed more time to sort things out.

Melanie's recent phone call had galvanized Kate's new game plan: find someone suitable to marry and with whom she could start a family. As soon as possible!

So that's why Kate, on this cold day in Manhattan, with a little light snow falling all around, found herself exiting the coffee shop just a block from Park Avenue on 23rd Street —trailed by Harry Winfield. They'd just completed their first meet-up, arranged through a dating app.

Harry was not much taller than Kate's five-foot-six. He had a pleasant enough face but that's not what turned Kate off as she glanced at her watch.

"So, coffee was fun. How about tomorrow night? A movie?" Harry asked.

"I'm sorry, Harry, but there's not going to be a second date."

There was an awkward pause.

“Why not?” Harry asked. “I thought we had a lot to talk about.”

“We did, and I’m grateful for that, Harry. But I don’t feel comfortable with the way you manipulated, even twisted, the truth.”

“What do you mean?”

“Well, in your profile description you say you’re six feet tall.”

“So?”

“So, I estimate you’re no more than five-foot-eight.”

“I rounded up.”

“And you said you were an entrepreneur and a computer programmer with ten employees reporting to you.”

“So?”

“But over coffee, you said you’re a cybersecurity expert working for a major security firm.”

“That’s close enough.”

“What about your age? In your profile you described yourself as in your late thirties. But over coffee, you confessed to being fifty-one.”

"That's not that much older than late thirties."

"I disagree."

After an awkward pause, Kate added, "And then there's the issue about the check."

"There was an issue?"

"Look. Harry. I'm a liberated woman. It's fine with me if you want us to split the check. But you asked me to pick it up because your credit cards are maxed out. I don't think I want to know that on our first date."

"But you just said you didn't think I was honest enough?"

"Look, Harry. I'm optimistic there's someone out there for you. It's just not me."

"But…"

"How could we ever have a relationship? Everything you put in your profile was misrepresented."

"I could learn to be honest," Harry replied. "You could teach me…"

Kate cut him off.

"I have to run, Harry. Thanks for meeting me. Sorry it didn't work out."

"Me too."

***

The door to the darkened apartment opened as Kate entered, followed by her best friend, Brenda, who lived just a block away. Brenda was scrolling through the dating app profiles on Kate's smartphone.

"You signed up for five dating apps?" asked Brenda.

"I thought I told you already. After my phone call from Melanie."

"Yes, you're right."

Brenda kept scrolling profile after profile.

"Does Jennings know?"

"Absolutely not!" Kate replied in a loud voice.

Brenda looked up.

"Are you gonna tell him?"

"Why? It's none of his business."

"But Kate. You've been dating him forever. Don't you think it's sneaky creating all these profiles and signing up for all these dating apps behind his back?"

"No," Kate said. "He put me on hold, remember? He said he 'needs more time.' His loss. I am a woman on a mission."

"And what mission is that?"

"I want to find Mr. Right and I want to start a family. If Jennings gets his act together, I'll delete all my profiles. But only if he asks me to marry him and really means it. But if he keeps dragging his feet, I have every right to date as many men as I want to."

"What if you meet someone you're attracted to? Will you tell Jennings?"

"Brenda, you're getting ahead of yourself. Let's see what happens."

"All right, then. So. How'd it go with that guy today, Harry?"

"You mean this afternoon. It was just coffee and it's a good thing. He was not my type. He didn't even match his profile."

"What does that mean?"

"Let's just say if this is what I'm going to find on the dating apps, Jennings won't have anything to worry about."

Kate dropped her oversized purse and her tote and peeled off her gloves and coat. *What will I tell Jennings if I find someone else?* Kate thought. She and Jennings had discussed dating others. Jennings always said he was too busy with work and Kate to date anyone else. And even though he'd put them on a temporary hold, Kate couldn't bring herself to tell Jennings about her dating app plans. She felt guilty going behind Jennings' back, but she also felt she had given him two years of her life. "Why ruin a good thing?" Jennings had said when Kate reminded him that their two-year anniversary was coming up and she wanted to get married. And "Why don't you just move in with me?"

"Don't you remember?" Kate protested. "I lived with my first husband for seven months. Then we got married and everything changed. So, this time, I'm trying a different approach. Dating and then marriage. No in-between 'playing house' stage."

"Kate, I'll tell you what's out there. Nothing!" Brenda said, interrupting Kate's thoughts. She went to the refrigerator for a beer. She popped open the can and took a long slug.

"There are no good men anymore," Brenda added. "At least not for beautiful, intelligent, successful women like us, and in our late thirties. The men in their thirties want women in their twenties.

And I don't want a man in his forties or fifties. They're too set in their ways by then or they've got kids from the first relationship that didn't work out."

"Look, Brenda, all I need is one."

"Plus batteries."

"Brenda, that might work for you, but I enjoy having a man to share my life with. I'm sorry my first marriage didn't work out but I was too young at twenty. And I'm sorry that Jennings has commitment issues. But I've learned from each of those relationships."

"Okay, I get it. When you find him, let me know so I can share him with you.

"That's not my thing, Brenda. Why don't you keep looking on your own?"

"It's exhausting. Between my job and walking Simon there aren't enough hours in the day."

"Listen, Brenda. Make yourself at home while I jump into the shower. I have another date tonight. This one is for drinks. The second shift. This guy sounds promising."

"That's what you said about the guy who turned out to be a lawyer for the mob. Where did they end up sending him? Was it Rahway?"

"It's not called Rahway anymore. It's East Jersey State Prison, maximum security. No, he got sent to Danbury. That's a federal prison."

"What a shame he got sent to prison. I really liked him, although I could see being a lawyer for the mob wouldn't be a very good connection to have for you and your clients."

"That's right!"

While Kate was in the shower, she called to Brenda, "Can you pick out a dress for me? I'm running a little late."

Brenda continued drinking her beer as she looked through Kate's wardrobe. She studied each of the tops, pants, jackets, and dresses in turn, muttering an occasional "no" or "yes" or "maybe."

"Here," Brenda said as Kate stepped back into her bedroom with an oversized towel wrapped around her and a second towel wrapped around her head in turban style.

"This is an interesting choice," Kate replied, staring at the jean jacket decorated with sequins and colorful appliques of flowers and animals.

"I like this look," Brenda explained. "It brings out the 'fun' side of you. Most of the time you're too much of an academic. I think the 'doctor' in front of your name, or the Ph.D. after it, scares away most men. You start talking about Emile Durkheim and his classic work on suicide and guys want to run for the hills."

"Point taken. But I'm just not into the 'hip' look tonight."

"Whatever. What's this one's name?"

"I have to look in my Excel spreadsheet to find it. He's date number twenty-seven. I know that but I don't remember his name."

"You'd better figure it out before you get to the bar where you're meeting."

"Absolutely. And can you hand me my hair dryer? I've got to get my hair as dry as possible before I head out into the cold."

"Sit down, my friend," said Brenda, lovingly. "I'll dry your hair for you!"

"You're the first girl I've let dry my hair since my sister Melanie and I lived together!"

"Thanks, my friend. I'll take that as a compliment."

Chapter 2

"Okay, here we go. Watch this and tell me what you think." Dennis Jacobs, a somewhat overweight, jovial man in his early forties joined his best friend and business partner, Joe Wexler, on the couch. Dennis clicked the remote.

The TV lit up, and a video monitor with color bars filled the screen, followed by the standard FBI warning about unauthorized copies. The scene shifted to a very messy living room and an unattractive woman dressed in flowery two-piece flannel pajamas, with pink hair curlers, seated on the sofa in front of an oversized flat screen TV. She was eating chocolate candy from an enormous box with one hand while picking dirt out of her toes with the other. She looked up and scowled.

"Where the hell have you been? You look terrible. I got tired of waiting for you, so I ate dinner without you, and you know I hate eating alone but I had to. I need some money. And somebody called about one of your credit cards getting cancelled. Did you forget to send in the payment again? Can't you switch to online billing? Get over here. Give your honey a foot rub."

An announcer stepped into the scene. He nodded to the mess behind him, saying, "Are you tired of coming home to something like this every night? Or something even worse?"

The camera flashed to show an empty room with dead plants, dirty dishes piled in the kitchen sink, and take-out cartons strewn around. A lonely man sat on the couch, head in hands.

"Gentlemen, your dreams have been answered," the announcer continued. "No more will you have to choose between a life of marital misery and a life of loneliness. Because now, for just twenty thousand dollars, you can have your own *robot wife*!"

On cue, the robot appeared on-screen. Joe had been careful about one thing: the robot wife he created wasn't supposed to look like a robot. Instead, he modeled her in every visible detail after Rosemary—blonde hair, flawless skin, a figure that turned heads—so lifelike that, at a glance, no one would ever guess she wasn't human. She even wore a dress, chosen to make her appear unmistakably human, as she crossed the room toward the man sitting alone on the couch.

“Darling,” the robot told him. “I’ve been counting the minutes since you left this morning. I miss you so much. I waited to have dinner with you.”

The lonely man perked up and followed the robot wife into a now-pristine kitchen.

The announcer stepped forward. “Yes, I know it’s too good to be true, and sounds like science fiction, but it’s real! Give your robot wife whatever name you like. Maria. Roberta. Sally. She will play chess, checkers, video games, poker—whatever you want. And you don’t even have to pretend to let her win! She’ll win all on her own. She will keep your home clean and tidy, be there when you want to talk—and leave you alone when you’re watching the game with the guys. Without complaining!

“What better way to end a stressful day? You can come home, kick off your shoes, curl up on the sofa with a good book, or listen to music, and relax with your robot wife.

“Call today! We are taking orders for next year’s model at this year’s twenty-thousand-dollar price point. Don’t delay! Almost sold out!”

The TV screen goes black. Dennis turns to Joe.

“What do you think? Will it grab men and motivate them to rush out and buy a robot wife?”

"Great commercial, Dennis! But whether it will encourage men to plunk down twenty thousand dollars is a question I can't answer right now. Also, don't you think the approach is a bit sexist?" And do we need to wonder about naysayers who believe AI robots are taking over so they no longer need a physical robot wife?"

"No!" Dennis exclaimed. "The commercial is supposed to be stereotypical and funny. Everyone will know the grouchy wife-bit is a satire or a spoof."

"Are you sure about that?" Joe looked unconvinced.

"Okay. Why don't we show the ad to Rosemary and see what she thinks?" Dennis suggested.

"Okay, I'll get her. But don't expect too much. She's got mixed feelings about being our prototype model."

Dennis nodded. "Sure, but she also gets a percentage of every sale so we're about to make her a very rich woman…"

"Only if we get enough customers, Dennis. We still need to pay down the development costs that we need to make the prototype."

"That's true."

"Rosemary. Can you come in here?" called Joe.

A gorgeous woman with blonde hair and a perfect figure emerged from the other room. She was wearing a stunning dress that made her look even more glamorous, like a movie star. Her gestures and stance, and the graceful way she moved, closely resembled those aspects of the robot wife in the video.

Dennis eyed her appreciatively and then turned to Joe. "Those programmers got it right. Who wouldn't want to come home to that!"

"Watch it," Joe snapped. "Rosemary, come see this, and tell us what you think."

Rosemary joined them on the sofa. Joe had hoped she would sit right up next to him but instead she perched on the edge. She seemed to be almost leaning forward as if she was eager to leave.

Dennis replayed the video.

"It's good," Rosemary said, when the commercial was done. "But isn't it a bit sexist?"

Dennis rolled his eyes. "I think it's absolutely brilliant. It's our ticket to millions of likes on social media and lots of sales. Let's see. To generate one million dollars, at twenty thousand dollars each, we only have to sell fifty robots."

“Are you sure about that?” asked Joe. “That seems like a very low number.”

“No. Do the math. Twenty-thousand times fifty is one million.”

“But what about production costs?” asked Rosemary.

“You’re right. Each robot costs five thousand dollars to manufacture and another thousand for life insurance.”

“Why does a robot need life insurance?” Rosemary asked.

“In case it’s destroyed or, worse, if it hurts someone. The life insurance also includes coverage if the robot trips someone and causes bodily harm.”

“What about investing in Match.com or one of the other popular dating apps?” asked Rosemary. “Isn’t a real woman better than a robot wife?”

“You’re missing the whole point,” said Dennis. “Besides, women today prefer their partners to do the dishes or to hire a cleaning service. Robot wife is old fashioned. She’ll still do all the domestic work without any resentment.”

“We just have to show the commercial in a few test markets and see what sales it generates,” said Joe.

“Great idea,” said Rosemary.

“I’m glad you see it that way, Rosemary. Because I have another idea. It’s an even greater idea.”

With that, Joe got down on his left knee in front of Rosemary, who was still sitting awkwardly on the coach. Dennis suspected what was coming so he whipped out his iPhone so he wouldn’t miss one moment of the exciting event unfolding.

Joe reached into his back pocket and removed a little dark blue velvet box. He quickly opened it up to reveal a diamond ring.

“Rosemary, will you marry me?”

Dennis kept filming as Rosemary blustered out, “No, Joe.”

Joe was stunned. He quickly snapped the box shut and scrambled to his feet.

“Why not?”

“Because I’m not in love with you.”

“But we’ve been dating for six months, and we seemed to be getting closer.”

“Joe, you might be in love, but for me, you’re a date, and a wonderful date, but I never said I wanted to spend the rest of my life with you.”

"But I thought when you agreed to be the prototype for the robot wife, knowing that would lock us in for life when the sales start and you get your commission on every sale, that you saw yourself as my partner in love and not just in business."

"Sorry to disappoint you, Joe, but that's not why I did it. I was flattered you asked me to be the prototype. Besides, if it takes off, it will make us a lot of money and who doesn't like to be part of something new, innovative, and lucrative. But that's what it's always been for me. A business venture. And you've been a fun date."

Joe sunk into an oversized chair. He didn't want to sit on the sofa next to Rosemary any longer.

There was an uncomfortable silence of several minutes.

"I think you should leave now," Joe said to Rosemary.

"I agree," said Dennis.

Rosemary stared at them with determination in her eyes.

"That's not possible," she said.

"Why not?"

"Because this is *my* apartment, so the two of *you* have to leave!"

"You're right!" said Joe, embarrassed by his confusion.

"The sooner, the better," Rosemary continued. "I feel very uncomfortable with our situation now that I've turned you down."

"Don't worry," said Dennis. "Joe is the gentlest, kindest man I know. He'll probably even forgive you."

"No, I won't," said Joe as he headed toward the bathroom.

"Where are you going?" Rosemary asked. "I've asked you to leave!"

"I need to get my toothbrush."

"Okay."

"What about the rest of my things?" Joe asked.

"You can send Dennis or one of your other friends to pick everything else up tomorrow. I'll pack it all up for you."

"You're being very cruel," said Joe.

"Please, Joe. This is hard for me. We want different things. You told me you want a wife and children. I want a career. I don't know if I ever want children. I wouldn't make a good mother."

"How do you know that?"

"I just know. I'm sorry, Joe. I really am. But your proposal actually came at a good time because I didn't know how to tell you that I needed to end things. I realized our relationship isn't working for me any longer. And it's not fair to me or to you. You deserve better. We both need to move on."

"Come on, Joe," Dennis interrupted. "My good friend, you're starting to make a fool of yourself. Rosemary is wrong and someday she'll regret what she's doing now. But for now, you've got to leave while you still have your pride and your dignity. Don't beg."

"Okay," Joe replied, reluctantly.

He finished retrieving his personal items from the bathroom, stuffed everything into his pockets, and walked out of the apartment where he had lived with Rosemary for the last few months for the last time.

They headed down the three flights of stairs to the main lobby and out the front door. Joe and Dennis stepped out into a snowy night. The snowflakes were thick and falling fast and furiously. The city was a sheet of white.

As he walked down the slippery snow-covered sidewalk, Joe almost fell. Dennis grabbed him.

"I got you, my friend," Dennis said.

Together they continued down the sidewalk with Dennis holding up Joe who, at six-foot-five, was a full head taller than his friend. They kept walking, leaving footprints in the snow.

Chapter 3

Just one day into December, the city was ablaze with multicolored lights and decorated store windows. A band of musicians sat in their bridge chairs in front of the supermarket on Third Avenue playing Christmas songs for free.

Joe barely noticed them. He made his way slowly, being careful not to slip on the occasional patch of ice. He wore a sad look on his face. The breakup with Rosemary was still very much on his mind.

As he passed a Santa ringing a bell, the Santa bellowed, "Merry Christmas, Merry Christmas, Ho, Ho, Ho."

"What's so merry about it?" Joe asked.

"It's that time of year," the Santa replied.

"What time is that?"

"The time to be grateful and joyful."

"And what if I don't feel joyful?" asked Joe.

"But you have so much to be grateful for," the Santa continued.

"What are you talking about?"

"Look down at your feet," said the Santa.

Joe stood for a moment and looked at his feet.

"Okay, I'm looking at my feet. So what?"

"Didn't your mother ever say to you, 'I cried because I had no shoes, till I saw the man who had no feet.'"

"No, my mother never said that to me."

"Well, she should have!"

With that, Joe tossed a dollar into Santa's donation kettle.

"That's it?" asked the Santa.

"I'm having writer's block," Joe replied. "It's all I can afford."

"Really?" asked the Santa.

Joe started to feel guilty. He reached into his wallet and pulled out a twenty.

"Here."

"That's much better," said the Santa.

"I'm glad you're pleased."

"But you didn't tell me what you want for Christmas," said the Santa.

Joe thought for a moment and answered, "How about a little privacy."

"You don't have to get rude about it!" the Santa replied.

At that moment, Dennis joined them. "What took you so long? It's freezing out here," said Joe. "I've been waiting for you, and I got into a somewhat disturbing conversation with this Santa. Cost me twenty-one bucks."

"That was generous. So, let's get out of here, and grab a drink."

"Sure. Where do you want to go?"

"I know a great place on Madison and Fortieth Street."

"Anything closer? It's snowing after all."

"It's not that bad," said Dennis. "We'll hop on the subway. It's right here."

"Okay," said Joe.

Dennis and Joe walked into the bar frequented by lots of Madison Avenue advertising types. It used to be a hang-out for journalists but after the *Daily News* closed its physical office in 2020, writers tended to hang out in bars closer to their remote offices.

Joe and Dennis sat at the bar surrounded mostly by men in business suits. There were women as well; some were in business attire while others wore festive holiday outfits, including somewhat tacky holiday sweaters with sequins and images of Christmas lights all over the sleeves.

Dennis ordered them both light beers, then said, “Know what our problem is?”

“What?”

“We’re trying too hard,” Dennis replied.

“You mean *you’re* trying too hard. I’ve given up, remember?”

“I’m talking about finding customers for our robot wife prototype. What are you talking about?”

“Sorry. I thought you were talking about me finding someone new after what happened with Rosemary.”

“Well, I do have some advice there as well. You gotta make them think you couldn’t care less.

Women go for that 'I don't give a damn' bad boy attitude. Turns them on. Really."

"But that's not me," said Joe.

"Look, that's what women want. Okay, you see that guy over there?"

Dennis was nodding toward a man who looked to be in his early fifties.

"Yes. What about him?"

"He has women falling all over him."

"How do you know that?"

"Because I've been in here before and I've seen him in action. They fall over him."

"Why?"

"Because he doesn't care!"

"That's it? That's the secret?"

"Oh," Dennis added, with a slight smirk, "he's also worth fifty million dollars."

Joe got a "I could knock you off your bar stool" expression on his face. But all he said was, "Forget it."

Joe turned and motioned to the bartender that he wanted another beer.

"Not right now," Dennis told him.

"Why not?"

"Because I made us a dinner reservation."

"Why?"

"The second rule. You should never pursue the opposite sex on an empty stomach."

"You really think we're gonna meet somebody tonight? At this bar?"

"Not with that kind of attitude we're not."

"But I don't want to meet anyone, Dennis. Not yet. I'm still getting over Rosemary."

"Joe, you have to take the power back. Find someone new! Show her what she's lost!"

"But I don't really want to meet anyone tonight. I don't even know if I want to meet someone, ever! I don't care anymore, okay?"

Dennis took a deep breath and said, in a louder voice, "I'm going to find you a woman tonight if it kills me."

"Why can't we just have a nice dinner? A little dessert. A little brandy."

"That's a start," said Dennis, "but I need you to get back to writing and working on our company. Our business bank account can't afford the luxury of you feeling sorry for yourself over this breakup."

"I need more time, Dennis," Joe explained.

"I know it's only been a week but you are sleeping on the couch in my living room is cramping my style! I can't really bring anyone back if we're doing the roommate thing."

"I didn't realize that," said Joe. "I'm very appreciative of your hospitality, Dennis. I don't want to be alone right now."

"I know. That's why we have to find you a new woman, so you don't have to find yourself a lonely studio that's overpriced, tiny, possibly even facing a wall, without any windows, and that you don't want to go home to anyway. Boy that's depressing. Is your depression contagious?"

As he uttered the last words, a server approached.

"Is this the Jacobs party?" she asked Joe.

"Does this look like a party to you?"

"Sir, do you want your table or don't you?"

"Sorry," Dennis said, frowning at Joe. "Yes, we do. My friend here is just trying to be funny. Joe, you go on, and I'll take care of the bar tab," Dennis said.

"Okay," said Joe, and followed the server across the floor.

Dennis waited as the bartender tallied up their tab. He happened to glance toward the entrance to the bar just as the door opened and Kate Hellman entered. Kate rejected Brenda's "fun" outfit suggestion for her. Instead, Kate was wearing a conservative business suit, but there was just enough of her black lace blouse showing to reveal her underlying femininity.

Too tall for me, thought Dennis. *But she might be just right for Joe.* He also knew, from his own romantic experiences, that the only cure for a broken heart was to fall in love again. And he needed that to happen for Joe, and fast, so they could get their business back on track.

The window of opportunity for the new robot wife was fast closing. Dennis heard there were several other robot spouses in development. He and Joe were slightly ahead of the curve in getting their prototype finished, largely due to their Made in America approach to development and production. They had had programmers and designers working for close to a year on their prototype at a factory just outside of Nashville, Tennessee. Everyone signed an NDA and, so far, their robot wife's unique capabilities had not been leaked. But it was just a matter of time before another robot spouse became available, and a price war was sure to follow.

Kate pulled out her smartphone and looked at the time. She bit her bottom lip as she realized she was fifteen minutes late. She put her tote bag with her tablet down on the bar as she called up the dating app on her phone, scrolling to the picture of tonight's first in-person meeting. She remembered that the date, number twenty-seven, had texted her that he would be wearing a dark suit.

"Dark suit, dark suit. There must be a hundred dark suits in here," Kate muttered out loud.

Dennis quickly paid for his bar tab and turned to Kate, who had her back toward him. He was trying to see over Kate's shoulder when she turned around, startled by this stranger's sudden closeness.

"Oh!" Kate shrieked, a little too loudly.

"Sorry!" said Dennis.

Kate stepped back as Dennis looked across the bar area and saw Joe not that far away, sitting at a table. Dennis thought for a few moments and then turned back to Kate who was still looking at her smartphone and mumbling something inaudible to herself.

Dennis continued staring at Kate as he thought to himself, *She's just Joe's type!*

Kate gave Dennis a suspicious look as she stared at everyone seated at the bar again.

"Looking for someone?" Dennis asked Kate.

"Huh?"

"I asked if you're looking for someone."

"What if I am?" asked Kate. "What's it to you?" she added, defensively.

"Sorry. I don't mean to pry. But what if I can help?"

"No, thanks," Kate replied, more politely.

"Listen. I come here a lot. I might know who you're looking for. There are a few regulars I might not know by name, but I would know him or her if you gave me a description."

"I doubt you'd know him," Kate answered. "He told me this was his first time here."

"Okay. But let me know who you're looking for anyway. I still might be able to help. Who is he?"

Kate gave Dennis another suspicious look. She was becoming more and more anxious and impatient as she was now twenty minutes late.

"It's actually none of your business!" Kate replied, somewhat adamantly.

"Oh, I see. Then this must be a blind date. This guy you're meeting. You've never met him before, right?"

"What makes you say that?" asked Kate.

"Dark suit?" Dennis replied.

Kate shook her head, yes.

Joe was staring at Dennis talking to a beautiful young woman.

What's he up to? Joe thought. *I'll kill him if he's trying to broker a date for me!*

Just then, Dennis must have said something to make Kate smile because she suddenly had a big grin making her more than just a pretty face. There was something about her that made Joe smile, too.

Maybe death is a little too harsh, Joe thought as he suddenly felt grateful his best friend was acting as a wing man for him.

Back at the bar, Dennis was trying to peek at Kate's smartphone screen.

"Stop that!" Kate said. "You can't read what's on my phone! It's against the law. ECPA. Electronic Communications Privacy Act. So please stop!"

"I'm just trying to help," Dennis explained. "I know you're looking for someone in a dark suit." He paused to take in the sea of dark-suited men in the bar. Then she turned and nodded at her phone. "A photo would help."

Kate held her phone out of Dennis's reach. "Except that we did talk on the phone so I would know what he sounds like."

"Or maybe not. Someone's voice over a cell phone versus in-person can be very different."

"That's true. But he described himself in his profile as over six feet tall. And handsome."

"Okay," said Dennis, trying not to snicker.

Kate looked over the bar again.

"I don't see anyone who fits that description exactly. I must have missed him. I guess he couldn't wait because I'm late, although I thought there was at least a fifteen-minute grace time allowed.

"Wait. I think I might know who you're waiting for. He's over six feet tall but he's wearing a maroon sweater. Maybe he decided to ditch the dark suit. Too corporate for a first date."

"Okay," said Kate. "That doesn't make any sense but I'm here now so who are you referring to?"

"Follow me," said Dennis as he picked up his half-glass of beer.

"Wait," Kate said. "Let me see some ID."

"Why?"

"Why else would I go anywhere with you? Even across the room?"

Dennis looked puzzled, but he showed her his driver's license. She typed his basic information into her phone.

"Lead on," she told him.

As Dennis and Kate arrived at Joe's table, Joe looked up at this woman he had been staring at for the last couple of minutes. She was even more stunning up close.

"Joe, this is—ah—"

"You're not him," said Kate.

"I'm not 'who?' asked Joe.

"You're not my blind date."

Joe suddenly understood the situation.

"Look, whatever he's paying you, I apologize. My friend means well."

"Paying me? What are you talking about?"

"Dennis, I'm ashamed of you. You didn't pay her yet?"

"Joe, this isn't the waitress."

"That's not what I meant, Dennis. I know you're desperate for me to get out of my funk since breaking up with Rosemary, so I figured you were arranging to pay this young woman to come over here and sit with me."

"Wrong!" said Dennis. "I'd never pay anyone to do that!"

"That's right," Kate chimed in. "He just asked me to come over here. He's been trying to convince me that you're my blind date. I was supposed to meet someone here from one of the dating apps I'm on."

"What?" Joe blurted out. "I can't believe you would have to be on a dating app! You're so beautiful. Men must be falling all over themselves trying to get a date with you."

Kate could feel her cheeks heating up as she blushed.

"I'm so sorry," Joe quickly added. "That was much too bold of me!"

"That's okay," Kate replied. "It's probably my fault anyway. I was fifteen minutes late. My date, his name is Frank, probably gave up and left when I didn't show up exactly on time."

"That's his loss!" said Joe. "I'd have waited for you! Well, at least twenty or thirty minutes."

"That's good to know!" Kate replied as she stifled a laugh. *This guy's funny,* Kate thought. "Since I have to warn you that I do have a problem with that. I tend to be chronically late. Well, at least by ten or fifteen minutes."

"Don't be so hard on yourself," said Dennis. "I'm not always that punctual."

"Me neither," Joe added.

"Thanks, guys, but you see I'm a time management consultant. So being late, even by fifteen minutes, doesn't speak well for my branding or my expertise. I need to be a role model for my clients."

"For starters, why don't you sit down and we'll discuss this!" Joe added. He leapt to his feet and pulled out a chair for her.

"Sounds like a great idea," said Dennis, as he tried to hide the smile that was forming on his face as he realized his plan was working.

"Sure," said Kate, removing her coat. "Obviously Frank gave up on me because I was late, so I have a little time to socialize."

"I have to hit the men's room," said Dennis. "I'll be back soon. I'll leave you to it."

With that, Dennis walked away, toward the restrooms, knowing full well he would stay in that room for at least ten or fifteen minutes while he let nature take its course. He hoped it would be a nice restroom and that there might even be a big, oversized chair that he could sit on to wait.

As Dennis walked off, Kate settled into her chair, with her back to the wall. She still wanted to be able to look out on to the bar and the other tables in the restaurant in case her blind date Frank was actually there.

"I always sit with my back to the wall," said Kate.

"Why is that?"

"One of the other areas I consult on is crime. And it's a habit that those who might be worried about their safety in public places tend to follow so they can see who's in a public place or who's entering it."

"You don't work for the CIA or the FBI or anything like that, do you?" asked Joe.

"No. I'm a college professor and like I said, I'm also a consultant."

"May I ask what courses you teach?

"Of course. It can vary each semester but usually I teach at least one or two sociology courses, such as Intro Soc or Family, and one or two criminology courses."

She gave Joe a playful wink.

"Would it bother you if I did work for the CIA or the FBI?" Kate asked.

"No, it wouldn't bother me. But I'd want to know."

"Ironically, if I did work for the CIA or the FBI, especially if this was our first meeting, I wouldn't be allowed to tell you! When they sent me an invitation to apply recently, via e-mail, that was one of the requirements if I were to apply for the job. That if I was accepted into either service, it would have to remain a secret from even my closest family or friends."

"Well, it's good then that you're not in the FBI or the CIA," Joe replied.

"So, tell me…"

"Joe. My name is Joe."

"All right, Joe. Why was your friend so eager to have us meet?"

"That's Dennis. He's not just my best friend. He's also my business partner. And a week ago, the woman I thought was the love of my life, with whom I had been living for six months, the woman who I proposed to, the woman who is the basis of the prototype for our new invention, broke up with me. I think Dennis thinks if I don't meet a woman soon, I'll do something desperate."

"That seems quite extreme to me!" said Kate.

"I'm not serious about that and Dennis shouldn't be worried. I'm absolutely not suicidal. I love life. I'm just broken hearted and when I'm sad like this, I can't take business meetings, I can't write and work on the press release for our invention. I just feel like hiding somewhere."

"I see," she said. Then added, "I'm Kate, by the way. Kate Hellman."

"Nice to meet you, Kate," Joe answered. They shook hands although the shake lasted somewhat longer than most initial handshakes should have lasted.

"If it's not too personal to ask, why do you think Rosemary turned down your proposal?"

"Yes, that is very personal but I'm okay with answering it. She said that she is one hundred percent focused on her career right now and she knew that I'm at an age and stage where I want to 'settle down' and get married and have kids. At least one kid."

"She told you that?"

"Yes, and I actually didn't know she felt that way until I proposed to her. I had a ring and everything."

"Did you get down on one knee?" Kate asked.

"Now we're getting a bit too personal."

"Sorry about that. I didn't mean to pry."

"Okay. I'll admit to it. I'm a romantic. And, yes, I did get down on one knee."

"I'm sorry Rosemary broke up with you and that you feel bad about it if she's the woman you wanted."

"Thanks for saying that. But Dennis has pointed out so many times that I am lucky to have found out now because no one should commit to a life with someone else who doesn't want that other person as badly as he or she wants the relationship.

"I know what you mean!" said Kate.

"Now that we're getting personal, can I ask you a question?"

"Sure. But I might not answer it!"

"Okay. Here goes. You're a beautiful woman. You're obviously successful with your time management and crime consulting and your college teaching position. You could probably have any guy you want, so why are you in a bar looking to find a blind date that you met through a dating app?"

"Okay. It's a long story but I'll try to keep it short. I've been dating this guy, his name is Jennings, for two years now. He keeps saying he needs more time to decide where our relationship is going, even though he's confident he's going to want to eventually get married, but he's not ready yet. I was okay with that for the longest time."

"You said it's been years?"

"Yes, that's right. Thanks for listening! Then, a few weeks ago, my older sister Melanie called to tell me that she's pregnant with her first baby. She and her husband waited almost fifteen years to start a family. I know it sounds juvenile and hard to understand but as long as my older sister didn't have a family, I figured I had all the time in the world. I had a brief first marriage that didn't work out, and some dates and romantic relationships over the last decade. But when Melanie told me she's pregnant, I got a baby hunger that is indescribable. And suddenly, for the first time, I felt old at thirty-eight."

"Thirty-eight? I wouldn't have thought you're a day over thirty-four," said Joe, trying to inject some humor into Kate's emotional self-disclosure.

Kate started to cry, not a big cry, but a soft cry with tears slowly rolling down her cheeks.

"Here," said Joe as he removed his handkerchief from his pants pocket and handed it to Kate. "It's clean."

"Thank you," said Kate. "This is so embarrassing. I'm sorry I'm getting so emotional."

"I understand. What your sister said caused you to reframe your reality and to see your life in a new way. It happens to all of us at various times. I think when Rosemary broke up with me it had the same effect. What do I want in life? Where am I going?"

Joe caught himself before he said too much, too soon in whatever this might turn out to be with Kate.

"Joe, I know we've just met, but is it too bold of me to ask what your relationship goals are?"

"No, that's not too bold at all. I'm forty-one and I think for me, it's important that I find Ms. Right and start a family. I want at least one kid. I'm curious about what that kid would be like, and I want to have the experience of sharing my life with someone and together creating another human being. Maybe even two or three."

"Wow! I've rarely heard a man articulate a need for offspring in the same way. I'm impressed."

At that moment, just as their conversation was getting more intimate, Dennis returned from the bathroom.

"How are you both getting along?"

"No complaints," Joe immediately replied.

"Ditto," said Kate.

"Well, I have to get going, Joe. I already paid the server so you two can sit here as long as you want. I'll be on my way."

"Call me later," said Joe.

"I'll do that."

Dennis made his way across the crowded floor. As he was exiting, a man in a dark suit who looked to be a little over six feet tall was entering the bar. Dennis had the instinct that he should confront him.

"Are you looking for someone?" Dennis asked.

"Yes, I am."

"First date? Blind date?"

"Yes. Maybe you've seen her? She's got brown hair and she said she would be wearing a dark business suit with a lace blouse.

"Yes," Dennis replied. "Someone like that was here a little while ago. She waited at the bar, but she said whoever she was meeting must have forgotten so she left. You just missed her."

"Oh no. Really? I didn't think I was that late," the man replied.

"I think she waited fifteen minutes."

"I thought twenty minutes was the grace period. Oh well. She couldn't have been that interested or she would have waited. Thanks, man, for letting me know."

"Yes."

"One more question, if I can boldly ask: was she pretty?"

"Not really," Dennis replied.

"Thanks again, man."

With that, the man from the dating app shook his head, turned around, and headed outside. Dennis glanced back at Kate and Joe who were still talking to each other, smiling occasionally. That led Dennis to smile at himself as he walked out into the snowy cold December night.

Chapter 4

Four hours later, the bartender announced, "Last call." Kate and Joe knew when they heard those words that they had less than an hour to drink up and to finish their conversation. Even though legally the bar could stay open until 4 a.m. in New York City, this bar was going to close by 2 a.m.

"What time is it, anyway?" asked Kate.

"I'll have to look at my watch," said Joe.

"I can't believe I haven't looked at my phone recently. That's the longest I've gone without checking my messages in ages."

"So, you're addicted to your smartphone?" Joe asked.

"Yes. I confess that I am."

"That's okay. Everyone's dealing with that these days. It's one o'clock now."

"Wow! I can't believe it's that late."

"How about I call you an Uber?"

"Sure. But let's do it right before we're ready to leave or it will be waiting outside too long."

"Okay. That makes sense. So, I have a few more questions to ask. How many dates have you been on through the dating apps?"

"I usually find around five or ten profiles I want to follow up on at each dating app. I'm on half a dozen apps, so that adds up to dozens of profiles. But I only keep track of how many first or second dates I've been on, rather than how many profiles I have.

"So how many first or second dates has it been?"

"Almost thirty dates, but no second dates yet."

"Wow! That's amazing."

"Amazing or discouraging? It's so time consuming! And with my consulting practice, and teaching three days a week in Westchester County, all my time is taken up with my search."

"Okay. I'm going to be very bold here. I don't suppose you'd like to go out on a date with me?"

"You're right. We haven't had a date yet! This was just a meeting!"

"Yes. It would technically be our first date."

"When?" asked Kate.

"How about tomorrow night?"

"Sorry, Joe. I already have a date lined up."

"Okay. Well, how about lunch, then."

"I have a date for lunch, too."

"Okay. Breakfast? I could do a breakfast date."

Kate shook her head. "Booked up for breakfast tomorrow as well."

"Kate, do you want to go out with me or not?"

"I do, Joe, but I told you. I'm on a mission to find a husband and start a family. So that's what I am devoting myself to, besides my jobs, morning, afternoon, and night, weekdays and weekends."

"I get it."

"Why don't you call me next week and we'll schedule something then," Kate added. "I enjoyed our conversation tonight so let's definitely get something scheduled."

"Next week?"

She's busy on her phone. Then looks up, all business-like.

"If next week doesn't work for you, things are so hectic around the holidays, how about after the New Year? I have an opening for a date the second week of January. Thursday, January tenth, at four o'clock."

Joe just stared at Kate. Maybe he had been misreading the strong "I could really fall for you" signals and vibes that she was giving out for the last few hours of their nonstop conversation. He learned they had so many things in common. They both loved to go to the movies. They both loved the theater and that was one of the reasons they loved living in New York City. Broadway and off-Broadway.

They discovered that they both loved occasionally going to a museum or art gallery. They both loved to travel. Joe had been to several countries in Europe, and he looked forward to exploring even more. He'd been to Australia once and wanted to go back there. Kate had done more traveling since she was invited to speak around the world but those were business trips. She looked forward to traveling with a romantic partner.

He stared at Kate in a way that filled her up all over.

"What?" Kate finally asked.

"I just want to see you. How about before your breakfast date, we grab a coffee?"

"*Before* breakfast?"

"Yeah. *Before* breakfast if that's what it's going to take to see you again!"

"Can you call that Uber for me now?"

"Sure," said Joe.

"Before breakfast tomorrow?" Kate repeated.

"Yes."

Kate took a deep breath and replied, "Okay. Meet me at Seventeenth and Third at six a.m."

"Six a.m. It's still dark then!"

"So, bring a flashlight."

"I've got one on my smartphone. Give me a minute," Joe said. He entered some information into his phone and then turned to Kate and said, "Your Uber will be here in four minutes."

"Okay."

"I'll walk you out."

"Thanks."

As they walked toward the front door, Kate asked, "You sure you want to do this tomorrow?"

"I'm sure. I've never been so sure of anything in my life!"

"Don't get so dramatic," Kate said, laughing.

Joe forced a smile, but he knew there was something deeper going on with him. Kate had brought up feelings that he had buried not just for the last week but for many months with Rosemary. He knew on a certain subliminal level that his feelings for Rosemary were one-way, but he didn't want to believe it. He ignored the warning signs.

It felt so genuine and exciting, but a little bit scary, to have such strong feelings for this woman he just met. Kate. Kate Hellman. Even her name made him tingle all over. He was glad he was wearing an overcoat because he could feel himself getting hard and it would have been embarrassing if she saw that through his pants.

Was this the dopamine effect that anthropologist Doctor Helen Fisher wrote about in her classic *Why We Love* book? He had read her research published in peer-reviewed articles in his college psychology course junior year of college, the same year her book was published. He had read in her book about the chemical and neurological reaction when a couple falls in love, but he had only wished he could feel that way, till now. These sensations that Kate had caused were powerful and overwhelming to Joe.

He helped Kate into her Uber.

"Get home safely," he said as he closed the door and the Uber drove off.

“What am I, nuts?” Joe mumbled to himself. This would be his first pre-breakfast date ever.

***

The next morning, at 6 a.m., a van was stationed at the corner of Third and Seventeen streets as several young men and women, all looking to be in their late teens or early twenties, filed into the vehicle. Kate was standing at the rear doorway, helping everyone up the high step, if they needed help, as Joe arrived by cab. It was easy enough to get a cab at 5:45 in the morning.

“Get in,” Kate said to Joe. “We’re running late.”

***

Around thirty minutes later, Joe found himself at a desolate strip of highway in the New Jersey wetlands. The van was parked along the cross as each person climbed out of the van in a single file.

During the trip, Kate explained to Joe that she taught Intro Soc and that these were her students, mostly first-year students but some sophomores, juniors, and even a few seniors. They were up to the chapter in the textbook where they were discussing the environment. She thought the best way for them to learn about it was to go on a field trip to see what happens to garbage after it’s thrown out.

"I went to college for four years," Joe said, "and not one of my professors arranged for us to go on a field trip."

"It takes a lot of time and effort to arrange it," said Kate, "but my students have shared with me, over the years, that it's their most memorable learning experience."

"I can see that."

"Unfortunately, I had to stop arranging field trips for a few years because of COVID but now I've started again, even for my remote classes. If the class is remote, of course the field trip must be optional. This Intro Soc class is remote. We meet through videoconferencing twice a week for an hour and fifteen minutes for each class. But this field trip, even though it's optional, got a sixty percent compliance rate. That's nine students plus us in the van out of a class of fifteen."

"Impressive," said Joe.

"I apologize in advance if I seem distracted on this trip," Kate explained.

"What do you mean?"

"Here's the thing. College professors are not by law required to act as 'mandatory reporters.' What that means is that certain caregivers, such as doctors or counselors, are mandated to report suspected child neglect or abuse. But the college where I teach requires me to be a mandatory reporter on field trips. Some of my freshmen students are minors, under eighteen. So, if I observe inappropriate behavior of any kind, even if it's between students, I have to report it."

"I see."

"So that means I have to keep my eyes on the students at all times. As well as on the reason we're here."

With that, Joe speared a disposable water bottle with a harpoon-like stick that Kate had provided and put it into a mesh bag.

"Joe, did you know that it is estimated that in the U.S. in just one year, fifty billion water bottles are consumed. Globally, it's estimated to be half a trillion water bottles! And most end up in landfills like this!"

"But what about recycling?"

"Good point. Thirty-three percent are recycled in the U.S., but it's said that only fifteen percent are recycled globally."

"So, what can we do?"

"Joe, that's why I take my students on this field trip. It shows them, personally and directly, just how many plastic water bottles end up in landfill.

"Solutions?"

"Switching to reusable permanent containers is one solution. But I know that's more time consuming because you have to refill it and wash it out. A better option might be to expand the bottle deposit program. Did you know that states that require consumers to pay a deposit on every plastic water bottle have seventy to ninety percent recycle rates compared to the much lower rates of no more than thirty percent?"

"You really know your stuff, Kate!"

"Thanks, Joe. In addition to educating my students, I'm trying to get the word out about this by working on my first documentary. It's going to be short. Under thirty minutes. The working title is, *Buried in Plastic: The Water Bottle Crisis* or an alternative title is, *The Landfill Lifespan: What Really Happens to Plastic Water Bottles*."

"Either title works for me! Kate, you know, I'm a writer as well as an inventor. I'd love to work on the documentary with you."

Kate stopped what she was doing as she stared right into Joe's brown eyes. "We'll see."

She turned away, and then she added, "That's actually a lovely thought."

"Thanks, Kate."

"Why are you thanking me?" she asked.

"You told me that you're a sociologist in addition to being a time management consultant. I always wondered what a sociologist does. Now I see one of the projects that a sociologist would tackle."

"Well, approaching the water bottle situation as a sociologist, since sociologists study group behavior, I'd want to look at the issue from that perspective as well. How can we modify group behavior to make recycling 'cool,' or to make having your own refillable water bottle as much of a cottage industry for unique designs and wording as the covers for smartphones?"

"Interesting."

"We sociologists have fun!"

"I see."

"Aren't you having fun?"

"Crawling through garbage on the side of the Jersey Turnpike. Going through the landfill to see what people throw away and where it ends up. It doesn't get any better or more fun than this!" Joe said, somewhat light heartedly.

"You wanted to go out on a date," said Kate, answering in a tone that indicated a bit of displeasure as she felt Joe wasn't thoroughly sharing in the excitement she felt about her work.

"I'm being facetious," Joe quickly added. "I'm also a little jealous. Since Rosemary broke up with me, I haven't been able to work, let alone feel excited by my work. Hearing you talk, listening to what you care about, and the way you bring not just time and effort but passion to your work, makes me remember when I used to feel that way about my work."

"I appreciate you admitting that. Not many men are in touch with their feelings to the extent that you seem to be!"

"Fourteen years of therapy will do that for you!" Joe replied.

"Fourteen years. That's a lot of years."

"It sounds like it, but it was only once a week although I also attended on a second night a group therapy session made up of six of the patients from my psychologist's individual sessions. That lasted fourteen years as well and for a long time, even after my psychologist died, we all got together as friends.

But that faded without our psychologist as the anchor."

"I'm impressed with your commitment to self-development."

"Yes, that's key for me," said Joe.

"Listen. I'd love to continue this conversation, but I must keep my eye on all these students, and I also must keep uncovering the secrets of waste disposal that are hidden in this landfill. 'You are what you throw out' could be the theme."

"I have work to do anyway!" said Joe as he speared another plastic water bottle and inserted it into the mesh bag, which was full to overflowing.

"Thanks. This will be an important sociological study someday," Kate added.

"I'm sure it will be!"

***

Forty-five minutes later, they were all loading up in the van, heading back to the Manhattan location where they had started their trip.

"Thanks for an interesting date," said Joe.

"I guess you could call it a date although it was a date with eleven people, plus the van driver!"

“I like your sense of humor,” Joe replied.

“Thanks! One of my secret goals is to become a standup comedian, even if I do it on the side.

“You mean like *The Marvelous Mrs. Maisel*?” asked Joe.

“Sort of but not really. I mean she had such a sad personal life in the series. I watched all five seasons! What about Season Four where Mrs. Maisel and Lenny Bruce get involved?”

“Yes, I watched, too. The real Lenny Bruce died at forty, a year younger than my age now, from an accidental overdose of morphine. He had such an unhappy life. So unfortunate. He was ahead of his time in so many ways.”

“Yes, I agree.”

“And what about the real-life sad story behind the actress who played *The Marvelous Mrs. Maisel*? Not her but her aunt, the late great Kate Spade.”

“You know about that?”

“Yes, I always admired her accessories. To die by suicide so young, at fifty-five. She seemed to have it all. Husband, daughter, career.”

“Rachel Brosnahan is the actress who played Mrs. Maisel, brilliantly I might add. So sad to lose her beloved aunt that way.”

“I agree,” said Kate.

There was a long awkward pause.

“Boy did we get sidetracked,” Kate said, suddenly.

“Yes, we did.”

“Sorry for the long silence. I guess being reminded of the heartbreaking fate of Kate Spade, especially since we share the same first name, hit me hard.”

“Sorry about that,” Joe said as he resisted the impulse to take Kate in his arms and give her the biggest hug she ever got and maybe even give her a kiss on the cheek. He knew they weren’t at the point of a tongue kiss although he had already been fantasized about that.

After a long somewhat awkward pause, Kate said, “Let’s get back to Manhattan. I’ve got a busy day ahead.”

“Yes, I know. You’ve got work and a couple of dates lined up.”

“You remembered.”

"I know that you're a woman on a mission and I respect and admire that! So when can I see you? I definitely don't want to wait until January tenth."

"Let me check my appointment book when I get back to my home office and let you know what we can work out."

"Okay."

"I really mean it. I'll check my book," added Kate as she wondered if her sincere practical requirement could be seen as pushing Joe away, which was not her intention.

"I understand."

"I appreciate that," said Kate, as she added, "Please call me. And I agree. Let's not wait till January tenth."

"What are you doing after breakfast?" Joe suddenly asked in a somewhat bolder voice.

"Are you serious?"

"Yes," answered Joe. "Absolutely. I could meet you *after* your breakfast date unless you have to teach a class or something."

"That's true but it would be rather awkward. Here's a better idea. I have a lunch date after the breakfast date, then a 'high tea' date with a man visiting on business from London but he swears he'll relocate to New York City if he meets the right one."

"Okay. Where do I fit in?"

Jennings's face flashed through her mind. She decided to ignore it. For now.

"If the 'high tea' date is a bust, I'll be free for dinner."

"How lucky can one guy get?"

Kate smiled.

"Do you want to meet me at eight o'clock at the Hudson Club?" Kate asked, somewhat flirtatiously.

"Sure. The Hudson Club at eight. Should I make a reservation?"

"If you're that confident." She smiled again. "Actually, that would be lovely."

"That means we'll be on our second date."

"Yes. You're right. You could consider it our second date."

"Did you figure out what number I am in your line up of dates on your mission?"

"I've decided that keeping track of what number date I'm on doesn't make sense in a certain way. After all, we just need one! But if you're determined to know that I think you'd be number seven-nine or maybe even thirty. I have to get back to my Excel spreadsheet to confirm that."

"But you're right about that!" Joe added, as he grinned. "What's the difference if someone's number one or number thirty. It's finding 'the one' that counts."

"Joe, by the way, thanks for joining me and my students this morning," Kate replied, switching the subject.

"My pleasure." Just as the cab was about to pull away, Joe called out the window, "Hey, Busy Lady! Was that eight a.m., or p.m.?"

"P.m.," Kate called back, as she suddenly found herself smiling in a way she hadn't smiled for a very long time.

Joe knew the next item on his day's agenda would be napping on Dennis' couch. It had been quite a morning, waking up in the dark at five a.m. to get dressed, grab his mandatory cup of bold black coffee, and meet Kate at 6 a.m. He was impressed by Kate's boundless energy. For now, he'd keep his desire for a nap to himself. He didn't want her to think he wasn't a good match for her in terms of their energy levels.

Chapter 5

Kate took a power nap in early evening, following her breakfast, lunch, and "high tea" dates, all of which were a bust. She didn't know if it was the field trip to New Jersey that had exhausted her, or all the emotions that this new guy from the bar, this Joe Wexler, was conjuring up in her.

Her feelings for Jennings had been more anger than passion lately. The Jennings situation was so complicated and frustrating.

So far, the situation with Joe has been pretty uncomplicated, although in the back of her mind she feared that this Rosemary he was still pining over might get back into the picture. Kate convinced herself she could not dwell on that now. She had to see where things might lead with Joe while still continuing to follow up on other profiles she had swiped as possibilities. She learned her lesson with Jennings. No exclusivity again until there was a ring on her finger.

As Kate prepared for her second date with Joe, she dried her hair using the blow dryer as a dance partner. Rock music blared from "Eiffel 65," an

Italian Eurodance group and one of her favorites, with their hit song, "Blue Da Ba Dee." It was Kate's song-of-choice to dance solo in her apartment.

When Kate turned off her hair dryer she heard her doorbell. Soon as she checked who it was and unlocked the door, her best friend Brenda barged in and headed straight to the refrigerator. Like a woman on a mission of her own, Brenda grabbed a can of light beer, popped open the can, and took a long swig.

Within minutes, Brenda guzzled the beer till it was empty. Kate just stood there, wondering what was driving Brenda to drink. Then Brenda took a second can of beer, popped it open, and repeated the whole process.

"Rough night?" Kate finally asked.

Brenda seemed to be ready to speak, but instead she took another long sip of the beer.

The next thing Brenda did was very out of character for her. Usually chatty, this time she walked to the open window in Kate's kitchen, the one that faced the courtyard of Kate's low-rise building in the middle of Chelsea, and shouted, "Argh! Millennials!"

"What's going on, Brenda?"

"Millennials," Brenda repeated, turning to face her friend. "I'd like to kill them all!"

"Watch what you say, Brenda," Kate responded, abruptly closing the window. "You never know who's listening or even recording us! And you can't just go around saying you want to kill people."

"Okay. You're right. And I don't mean I literally want to kill all Millennials. I'm just so frustrated and fed up with dating Millennials with commitment problems.

Brenda walked over to Kate's kitchen table, which also doubled as the breakfast and dinner table, and took another swig of beer.

"I need a nice, older man," Brenda said. "Someone who's housebroken. —Hey, since things aren't working out with Jennings, can I have him? I'll keep him company until he's ready to settle down."

Kate thought about the last conversation she'd had with Jennings. "Take a breath," Jennings had responded when she again told him she needed to know if and when he might completely and legally commit to their relationship. "I care about you, Kate, but I'm not ready. Maybe we just put things on pause for now?" Jennings suggested and Kate agreed.

She shook off her reverie and refocused her attention on her friend. "Jennings and I are still a possible something," Kate said. "So, no, you can't have him, Brenda, at least not yet. I'm still sorting him—things—out. But tell me what happened. Why are you so upset?"

"Okay. So, you know Susan, right? We went to this new club up in the nineties. I swear, we were the oldest people there. I mean old by about ten years. They were all in their twenties, barely old enough to legally drink. I felt ancient."

"What about the guys?"

"That's the point. The guys, the Millennials, they were all in their thirties and early forties, but they didn't notice me or Susan. They looked the other way. They were totally focused on the twenty-year-olds!"

"So, what did you do? Did you leave?"

"I wanted to. But Susan finally hooks up with one of the guys that she meets there. He's a Wall Street type, right? And before I know it, she's going off with not just one but two of them into some back room. I figure Susan can take care of herself. She's a big girl. But then I notice these other two guys are laughing at the situation, so I figure I'd better follow her, so I do. So, it's fortunately not some kind of sexual assault situation but instead she's engaged in a threesome, and it's obviously that she's absolutely loving it! And then she even asks if I'd like to join the party. So, she opens up a bag and she says, 'Look at all the coke.' And I check out the bag of powder and they all start laughing. It's not coke. It's artificial sweetener. The joke was on me. I wanted to kill them."

"So, then what?" Kate asked.

"What do you think, Kate?"

"I have no idea, Brenda!"

"Of course I joined the party!"

Kate laughed. "I wouldn't have guessed that. Good for you, I say. Beats sitting alone in your apartment, doesn't it?"

"Damn right!" Brenda replied.

"So why are you so upset?" Kate asked.

"Because these guys were just playing with Susan and me. When they do want to settle down, they're going for the Twentysomethings or the Gen Zs. The ones with younger chromosomes!"

"That's ridiculous!" Kate replied. "Didn't your mother have you when she was forty-four?"

"Yes," Brenda responded. "They always referred to me as their 'change of life baby.'"

"Tough label to have, I would assume."

"You said it!" Brenda answered.

"So, the bottom line is that despite everything, you and Susan had a foursome and a rollicking good time!"

Brenda took another drink of her beer.

"I guess you could look at it that way. Kate, you're always looking at the glass that's half-full."

"And you're always looking at the glass that's half-empty!"

"You're so right," Brenda replied as she began to cry softly. "How do I become more positive? I know being negative is a turnoff, especially on a date. *If* I go out on a date."

"I'd love to get into a discussion with you about self-love and all that, Brenda, but I have a date and I have to finish getting ready."

"Another one? Who's your date with, if you're okay with telling me? Is it Jennings?"

"No, it's that guy I met at the bar and grill by accident recently."

"You're going out with a guy you just fell into randomly at a bar and grill? What do you know about this guy, anyway?"

"I know his name is Joe Wexler and that he's a writer, an entrepreneur, and an inventor. I can't tell you about his invention just yet because he had me sign the NDA clause that everyone has to sign because it won't be available to the public until after January first. But it's going to be big. I know it."

"Oh yeah? I've heard that before from so many guys. The dreamers. But what else do you know about him?"

"I of course Googled him."

"But did you also do a criminal background check? Susan told me she's glad she did a criminal background check on this guy she met through one of the dating apps. It turned out, not only was practically everything he told her a lie, but he did time for burglary when he was nineteen. It was in his public record and because he was over eighteen, it wasn't sealed."

"No, I didn't do a criminal background check on Joe Wexler, but I learned enough from my Google search and his LinkedIn profile that I feel confident he's not an ex-felon. And besides, I'm not saying that he is, but you know I sometimes teach penology, and one of the evidence-based issues I talk about is the need for second chances especially for non-violent offenders."

"Okay, okay, Doctor Hellman! I didn't mean to get you off on your sociology/criminology tangent. If we do that, we could be talking all night, and you said you have to get ready for your date. I was just making my point that you shouldn't be so trusting."

"And you shouldn't be so judgmental, or you might find yourself still single and alone in twenty years!"

"That's a cruel thing to say," Brenda replied, holding back her tears.

"You're right. I'm sorry. I'm stressed over this date so forgive me, my friend.

"Why are you so stressed? You've been out on, what, twenty, thirty dates in the last few weeks?"

"I don't want to jinx things, Brenda, but I'm feeling things for this guy that I don't think I ever felt for Jennings."

"Listen," said Brenda, lowering her voice. "I suggest you hold on to those feelings but reserve judgment till you've been to bed with him. That's an important part of any relationship, as you know, and you don't know if he can cut it in that area."

Kate thought her best friend was being crude. On the other hand, what flashed through her mind were the couple of men that she'd sincerely fallen for years ago, both of whom couldn't perform to her satisfaction in that area. She was so lucky she found that out before things had gone further. For one of the guys, she'd realized after a few dates that he likely would not pursue the possible surgeries available to increase his length.

Then there was the bestselling author that she'd fallen head over heels in love with just months after her divorce a little over a decade ago. They dated for several months but the physical part of their relationship was never that satisfying. He had emotional issues that stopped him from allowing himself to enjoy sex. His wife had died at a young age from a brain aneurysm and, every time that he and Kate made love, his guilt over having another romantic relationship shut him down. It had been a few years since his wife died but everyone's grief and everyone's path from loss is unique. The timing was off for him and Kate.

Brenda and Kate shared pretty much everything with each other including the details of past romantic relationships. There was a girl code, however: you don't share the intimate details about a current romance, so Brenda was clueless about what Jennings was like in bed. She knew he had to be satisfactory enough that Kate had stayed with him for almost two years and that she did want to make a lifetime commitment to him, if Jennings agreed.

"Well, Joe and I are calling this our second date but it's actually our first real date. The last time we got together, if you discount the night we met at the bar and grill and talked for several hours, was when he accompanied me on the field trip to the landfill site in New Jersey."

Brenda took another swig of beer.

"The main difference between you and me, Kate, is that I know I'm never going to meet Mr. Right. But you. You still believe in the fairy tale."

Brenda finished her second beer and dropped the empty beer can into the trash can under the sink.

"I hate to say this to you, my dear friend, but you're just jealous."

Brenda ignored Kate's comment and instead, opened up the refrigerator.

"You're out of beer."

"Duly noted," Kate replied, relieved that her friend was either ignoring her comment about being jealous or she hadn't heard it in the first place.

"I gotta go, Kate. Susan found another place downtown that she said might have a better crop of potential dates or mates for us. I want to change into something a bit sexier before we head there."

"Good luck," Kate said as her friend reached for the doorknob.

"Tomorrow's a big day for me as well," Brenda added.

"What's up?"

"I always read the obituaries in the *Times*. If the age group is right, and the funeral is nearby, I show up in case the widower or one of the mourners could be a good prospect.

"I don't know if that's creepy, or ingenious," Kate said, giving her friend a hug. "Remember, Brenda, I really do think Mr. Right is out there waiting for you."

"Okay Ms. Pollyanna! I'll keep trying."

***

As Kate continued getting ready for her eight o'clock dinner date with Joe, Joe and Dennis were meeting at a local coffee shop. Joe wanted to talk about what was going on in his life, outside of the apartment they were sharing.

"Why all the cloak and dagger mystery?" asked Dennis. "Why couldn't we just sit down in the living room and talk?"

"You mean the living room where I'm sleeping on your uncomfortable couch?"

"Uncomfortable couch? That's the gratitude I get for giving you a place to stay after Rosemary kicked you out!"

"Okay, okay."

Joe had intentionally got them a booth by the window. It was his favorite coffee shop in Tribeca. He loved sitting by the window and watching all the people stroll by. Some were dragging Christmas trees as they made their way to their apartment, car, or the subway. Joe thought about the decorating and the merriment they had in store.

"Are you okay?" Dennis asked Joe. "You look strange."

Joe stared at his best friend. They met a decade before when they were both starting their entry level jobs at an advertising agency in midtown. Dennis had an undergraduate degree in philosophy from Princeton and a graduate degree, an MBA, from Duke. Joe had a BA in writing from The New School and an MFA in Creative Writing from NYU. They became fast friends, which led to being roommates for a couple of years, until they both made enough money to have their own apartments.

But their friendship continued even after they both left that initial agency and found work at other companies. Then, around four years ago, Dennis asked Joe to have a drink and suggested to his longtime friend that they start a company together. At that point, he didn't know what they'd do but Dennis knew he was tired of working for other people.

"If I don't start my own company now, in my thirties, I'm never going to do it," Dennis explained.

He had saved up enough money to cover all the initial expenses of forming an LLC, printing stationery and business cards, and purchasing a private mailbox at a local UPS store so they'd have a real street address, not just a P.O. Box number, until they could finance an outside office or even shared office space.

Joe agreed. They both quit their jobs, brainstormed what they could do that wasn't currently available, hired computer programmers and designers to help them make their robot prototype, using Dennis' initial investment, and then COVID hit. So, for a few years, the company was dormant as they both got by on freelance writing and editing gigs.

But after the COVID interruption, they went back to their original goal and their $20K robot wife concept took off. The prototype was so popular that they even managed to raise $20 million in venture capital funds toward the manufacture in Nashville of this amazing and unique robot. Nothing was stopping them from finalizing everything until the Rosemary/Joe meltdown.

Fortunately, Rosemary, who was used as the model for the robot, wasn't going to pull out of the venture completely, even though she and Joe broke up. Joe had told Dennis he needed some time before he could draw up the distribution and promotion plans that they would use to launch the robot wife after the New Year. But today he had something different to talk about.

"I don't know if I look strange," Joe began. "But I know I feel strange."

"Do you think you got COVID again?"

"No, Dennis, it's not physical."

"What is it then?"

"Well, it actually is partially physical. But it's physical in a different way. In a positive way."

"Tell me more, Joe."

"I think I'm in love with her."

"I know you're in love with Rosemary. But she threw you out. You have to accept that it's over. I'm sorry you still love her.":

"No, Dennis, I'm not talking about Rosemary."

"You're not? So, who are you talking about?"

"Kate Hellman."

"Kate? You mean the woman you met at the bar and grill? The one I introduced you to?"

"Yes, that woman. And I hold you responsible for my condition!"

"Me?"

"Yes. Because you introduced me to her! And you know what's really amazing?"

"What?"

"I'm writing again!"

"What!"

"Yes, Dennis, my writer's block has lifted." Joe held up a couple of pages. "This is the business, distribution, and marketing plan for our robot wife invention. The plan you've been asking me to put together for weeks now."

"You're kidding me? You actually wrote it?"

"I did, and I did it without any help from AI!"

"That's great, Joe," said Dennis.

"And guess what? I'm even working on a novel. You know that's always been my dream. That's why I went to graduate school in creative writing. But I always had excuses about why I couldn't write my novel. I was too busy with work. I didn't think my idea was good enough. I hadn't been struck by the muse."

"Yes, I've heard it all from you over the years."

"Well, the muse has struck, and her name is Kate Hellman."

"Aren't you giving this woman you just met too much power?"

"What do you think? Here it is. The first chapter. It's about a homeless couple who live along the New Jersey Turnpike. They live off the stuff that other people throw away. My working title is *Junkyard Juliet and Turnpike Romeo*."

Dennis sipped his coffee. "What about *The Great New Jersey Turnpike Romance*? Or maybe *Love in the Lost and Found Lane*?" Dennis suggested.

"Okay. Now I think you're making fun of me!" said Joe.

"No, my friend," said Dennis. "I think it's great and your novel certainly has promise. But are you sure what you're feeling is love? Maybe you're getting the flu?"

With that last comment, Joe realized something that anyone who's ever been in love, real, deep, once-in-a-lifetime kind of love knows that no one else really understands. That feeling is so strong and powerful and it scares not only the two lovers, but it seems to push everything and everyone else in their lives away.

"If only I could bottle how I'm feeling and if only we could sell it. We'd be millionaires, no, billionaires."

"I'm happy for you," Dennis said, as he stared out the window. He was trying hard to hide his jealousy.

"I know what you're thinking," Joe said. "I said the same thing about Rosemary several months ago."

"Yes, that's *exactly* what I'm thinking."

"But it wasn't the same, but I didn't know it at the time because I had never felt this way before. Not about Rosemary and not about anyone else."

"I gotta go," said Dennis. "Keep me posted! You said you have a date with this Kate later?"

"Yes, our second, but really our first official date. We're going to the Hudson Club."

"Have fun, and I hope the feeling lasts."

Chapter 6

Kate arrived at the Hudson Club a few minutes early so she would have time to go to the ladies' room and freshen her makeup. It was a magnificent room, with marble sinks and oversized chairs in the large secondary room that served as an entranceway to the toilets.

The toilet paper was soft and three-ply. That's how Kate knew it was a five-star restaurant. She also liked that everything was touch-free: the water faucets, the liquid soap, and the electric hand dryer that replaced paper towels. Kate could never understand why bathrooms might have only one or two of those three necessary elements when having all three made it one hundred percent germ-free.

She looked in the mirror. With her thirty-ninth birthday fast approaching, Kate still had very few lines or wrinkles on her face. There were one or two gray hairs but nothing to worry about yet. Her chestnut brown hair was thick and below shoulder length. She had thought of cutting it recently but whenever she went to the hairdresser, even if she just wanted a trim, they cut off too many inches and she regretted it. So, she just let it grow, and now it almost reached her waist.

She looked in the mirror and wondered how men felt about turning forty. As a sociologist who was all too familiar with the life expectancy tables from her Health and Medicine discussions in either Intro Soc or the Sociology of Health classes, she knew that forty was truly the beginning of middle age if the upper limit was eighty.

She reminded herself that "forty" was a generality and an oversimplification. Someone could live to ninety, or one hundred, so then it would not be middle age until fifty. Or someone could die from an accident, homicide, or illnesses at twenty, thirty, or sooner.

Whenever Kate thought about aging, she remembered her first cousin, Jerome. They were very close growing up even though there was a five-year age difference. He was her mother's sister's only child. He was a very bright and creative boy who'd taught her how to juggle three balls at once. He'd fallen off his bicycle when he was twelve. Hit his head. Wasn't wearing a helmet. Had a headache but no one thought anything of it when he took a nap.

But he never woke up.

She made a promise to Jerome when she attended his funeral. She stood at his open casket, looked into it, and declared, "Jerome, I'll never lie about my age. Every year is a blessing."

It was getting harder and harder to keep that promise as she approached forty and when she'd meet men in their thirties or early forties who might be a possible romantic partner. She knew being able to say she was closer to thirty-five would make her more attractive to them. She caught herself lying once on a date. He was tall, dark, and handsome, yes, and he was thirty-seven and looking to get married and to start a family. His parents had money but that wasn't something that Kate cared about. They lived in Kings Point, a little-known wealthy community near the more well-known Great Neck Estates. She was more interested in their son's intelligence and character.

Kate found herself lying when they first met at a mixer that his parents put together for the grown children of their friends from university. She said she was thirty when she was already thirty-five at the time. They dated for six months before she went to Europe for a week and he took that time to cheat on her. It had been such a burden keeping that lie for six months, she was almost relieved when he turned out to be a cheating jerk after all. In hindsight, Kate decided it wasn't worth the stress of lying. She tried to always remember that experience since then when she was tempted to lie opting to admit to her actual age, preferring to face any consequences.

She touched up her lipstick with her favorite, "Love that Wonderful Red." She stared in the mirror. *I'm thirty-eight years young*, she reassured herself.

Kate left the bathroom feeling more confident. She planned to talk about with Joe about theater and movies and fun things. She was going to stay clear of politics although it was something she'd want to know about before—if—they made a long-term commitment to each other. She was also going to steer clear of discussing religion, even though they already had established that they were both spiritual and they both had their religious upbringing, but it wasn't a deal breaker for either of them. They were both willing to "go with the flow," as they say.

Joe was already sitting at the table when Kate went to the front desk and asked about their reservation. It wasn't one of those restaurants that wouldn't let any of the party sit unless the entire party was present.

The hostess showed Kate to the table toward the back where Joe was seated.

He stood up as soon as he saw her. He got out from behind the table and walked over to Kate, pulling out her chair so she could sit down.

"You look lovely this evening," Joe said, with a smile.

"Thank you."

There was an uncomfortable pause.

"You look nice too," Kate blurted out, filling the silence with words.

"I appreciate that," Joe replied.

They both studied the menu as if they were taking a final exam in college. Kate knew it was just an excuse for her to do something with her hands and her mind since she was feeling quite nervous. She didn't know why she was so nervous. She'd been on dozens of dates. Why should this one be any different?

"Shall we order?"

"Great idea," Kate answered as she looked over the menu.

"Do you see anything you like? I've never been here before, so I don't have any recommendations."

"I'm a lacto-ovo-vegetarian so I'll probably look at the pasta dishes, some of the salads, or even some of the side dishes."

"What's a lacto-ovo-vegetarian?" Joe asked. "I've heard of vegetarians and I've heard of vegans, but I haven't heard of a lacto-ovo-vegetarian before."

"It just means that although we don't eat meat, fish, or poultry, we do eat cheese, milk and eggs. Dairy products."

"Thanks for that explanation!"

There was another uneasy pause.

"Will it offend you if I eat meat or fish?" Joe asked.

"No. I'm used to it," said Kate. "My best friend Brenda is a carnivore. We eat out all the time, and she always eats meat, fish, or poultry in front of me. I just tune it out."

Jennings never asked her if his carnivorous diet offended me, Kate suddenly found herself thinking.

Joe considered for a moment and then he said, "I think I'll have the pasta with marinara sauce and a side salad."

"Is that because of me?"

"If I say, 'yes,' is that okay?"

Kate blushed.

"Of course."

Even though the restaurant was busy, the acoustics were such that they could talk easily. They did not talk as long as they did that first night together in the bar and grill, but they did talk for over an hour. Kate felt comfortable enough that she even ordered cheesecake for dessert. She did not have to act as if she never ate sweets. Fortunately, she was the perfect weight for her height, but she knew that having a nice figure was something that helped her dating options. She did not take that for granted.

The evening was still young and the weather, although chilly, was not too cold for a walk in the holiday-filled city. They both bundled up in their winter coats, hats, and gloves as they strolled a few blocks from the Hudson Club to the South Street Seaport.

"Would you like to go into some of the shops and look around?" Joe asked.

"Sure. Why not?"

From there, they walked all the way to Chinatown on Mott Street.

"How about checking out the River Café overlooking the East River? I've heard you get a magnificent view of the city's skyline from there," Joe added.

I could get used to this kind of date, Kate thought to herself.

"Sure," said Kate.

Instead of waiting for an Uber, after around an hour at the River Café, Kate asked Joe if he'd like to go back to her apartment for a night cap.

"Why not?"

They agreed that they were fortunate that the third cab that went by had its availability light on.

It was Friday night at midnight. By this late hour the city traffic, even at this festive time of year, was winding down.

The cab pulled up in front of Kate's apartment building and Kate got out.

"Aren't you coming?" Kate asked.

Joe wanted to give Kate a chance to back out of her offer, but she extended it again.

"Of course. Thanks."

***

Kate waved to the friendly doorman as she and Joe made their way to the elevator as they took it in silence up to her floor and then to her apartment door. Her building had installed one of those keypad front door locks. She was so nervous she had to put the code in three times before she entered everything correctly.

"Sorry about that," Kate said.

"No apology necessary!"

They entered her darkened hallway. Kate never left a hall light on which she regretted now. It would have been nice to enter an apartment that already had at least a small light.

"I meant to leave the light on. Sorry about that."

"Again, no apology necessary."

Kate wandered into the kitchen off the front entranceway.

"Can I make you a cup of tea? Offer you a brandy? White wine? Red wine?" Kate asked.

"I'm fine."

Kate took a deep breath. She met Joe on December first. That was five days ago. Even though this was only their second official date, he did go on that field trip with her, and she hadn't stopped thinking about him ever since, in between all the other dates that she had.

"I don't want you to think I'm the kind of girl who has sex on the second date," Kate said, demurely.

"I wouldn't think that," said Joe.

"But I want to."

"Oh," was all that Joe could manage to say. He already had told his best friend that he thought he was in love with Kate so her admission, although a pleasant surprise to Joe, was not as much of a surprise as his declaration had been to Dennis.

"I'm certainly up for it, Kate. I have a confession. I haven't been able to stop thinking about you since we met."

"That's great! Me too! But there's something we have to do first."

"Before we have sex?"

"Yes. Trust me," said Kate. "I know it's not the most romantic thing to do, but it's the scientist in me."

"I trust you implicitly and completely."

"Great."

Joe remembered previous girlfriends who had their distinct ideas about making sex more fun.

Everything from asking him to dress up like a waiter, to keeping the lights on, not off, during lovemaking.

"Fortunately, there's a twenty-four-hour drug store on the corner. Grab your coat," Kate said.

Joe had a condom on him at all times, just in case, but he didn't know if it had expired, if there were even expiration dates on condoms, and he also was afraid to mention it. It might look too presumptuous.

"Sure. Let's go."

Within minutes, they had both gotten their coats, hats, and gloves on, and they were out the door. Within just a few more minutes, they reached the all-night drugstore on the corner.

Kate walked up to the pharmacy window and asked, in a whisper, "Where do you have your OTC instant STD tests?"

"I'm sorry," said the young woman behind the counter. "I can't understand what you're saying."

Kate repeated herself in a slightly louder voice. This time, she added more information in case that was the issue.

"Where do you keep your over-the-counter instant tests for HIV, syphilis, and other STDs?"

"Oh, thanks, now I can understand you. Over there. Right near the condoms."

"Thanks. That was going to be my next question," said Kate.

Joe stood in awe of Kate as she gathered up the STD quick test and a packet of six condoms. He liked her way of thinking. Be prepared and also be safe.

They immediately rushed back to the apartment.

"I've actually never done one of these quick tests before, but I've done the research. It just takes twenty minutes," said Kate.

"How about we listen to some music and relax while we wait for the test results?" asked Joe.

"Great idea!" said Kate.

"How about I pour us both a glass of wine," said Joe.

"Another great idea!"

While Joe poured the wine, Kate found her love song playlist.

"I have two playlists," Kate said. She intentionally left out the word *love*. "One's a more general play list and the other is more for Valentine's Day."

"Let's go with the more general one," said Joe.

"Sounds good to me."

The first song on the playlist was a bit melancholy, but Kate felt it fit her mood. *Grow Old Along with Me* sung by Mary Jane Carpenter.

"It's so ironic that one of the last songs that John Lennon wrote before he was murdered was this one, *Grow Old Along with Me*. He wrote it in 1980, before I was even born. They say he recorded it as a demo while in Bermuda. Although it's attributed to Lennon, it is said that he was inspired by a Robert Browning poem."

"That's amazing!"

"Here's something more amazing," said Kate. "I have memorized the entire first stanza of the poem by Robert Browning that inspired John Lennon."

"Would you recite it for me?" asked Joe.

"Really?"

"Absolutely!"

"Okay. It's from the poem *Rabbi Ben Ezra* by Robert Browning, first published in 1864. Here it goes:

Grow old along with me!

The best is yet to be,

The last of life, for which the first was made:

Our times are in His hand

Who saith "A whole I planned,

Youth shows but half; trust God: see all, nor be afraid!"

"That's absolutely beautiful, Kate!" said Joe.

"But now I'm sad," whispered Kate.

"Sad because of the poem?"

"No, sad when I think about John Lennon and his murder. He was only forty years old. I'm turning thirty-nine in a few days! Just a year younger than John Lennon's age when he died. I wasn't even born when he died but his music and his death have left such an indelible impression on me."

Joe couldn't help but put his arms around Kate and fortunately she didn't pull away.

"I feel the same way," said Joe.

After a few moments of silence, Joe said, "Can you play that song again? It's beautiful and I see it as more hopeful than sad. John Lennon left us a gift for all ages. He would not live to enjoy old age with his wife Yoko Ono, but he knew that was the ultimate gift any couple could have. It is what I dream of for my life. Growing old with that one person who cherishes me above all others."

Kate had to wipe the tears from her eyes.

"How about we check out the test results?" Kate asked, almost relieved to change the subject.

Joe looked at his smartphone. He had set the timer for twenty minutes.

"My phone says we have another seven minutes to go."

"Okay. But let's listen to a different song instead."

Kate turned up the volume on her smartphone so *Make You Feel My Love* by Adele played from its link to YouTube.

Joe felt his emotions swelling up so forcefully that he gently took Kate's hand and they started dancing in the living room area off her kitchen. They started somewhat far apart but by the time the four-minute song was over they were hugging each other tightly. Joe felt it was time to give Kate a kiss. First on the cheek and then he gave her a French kiss.

They kept dancing until the end of the song.

"I think it's time to check those results," said Kate.

Just then, Joe's iPhone alarm went off declaring that twenty minutes had officially passed.

Kate checked the quick test.

"What's the verdict?" asked Joe.

"We're good!" said Kate.

"That's excellent news."

With that, Joe took Kate's hand and he walked her ever so slowly into her bedroom.

"Is this okay with you?" he asked Kate.

"Absolutely," Kate replied. "Thanks for asking."

***

Morning came too soon for the happy couple. Their intimate embraces and connecting in the ultimate way were everything both of them had dreamed and hoped it would be. Everything about their first erotic encounter was perfect. They liked each other's aromas. The pacing was just right. They were concerned about each one being satisfied. It wasn't too quick or too slow. They even slept together without intruding on each other's space.

"Coffee?" Kate asked as her alarm sounded at six a.m. It was still dark outside. It was the snooze alarm since her original alarm went off at five a.m. Joe sleepily opened his eyes and felt surprised to see she was already dressed.

"Is it ready?" Joe asked.

"Yes. How do you take it?"

"Black. Two sugars. I mean two sugar substitutes."

"Coming right up."

Joe smiled as he thought about the wonderful day together that he planned for them. So many museums they might explore or maybe they could even do some Christmas shopping. "What about trying out the skating rink at Rockefeller Center?" asked Joe.

"Sorry but we have to get out of here very soon. I have an appointment this morning that I can't miss."

Instantly Joe went from being on cloud nine to worried.

"Another date?"

"Yes, but not the kind you're thinking."

"No pressure. Share whatever you feel like sharing."

"Thanks for understanding. How long will it take you to get dressed? I have an Uber coming in ten minutes."

"I can get dressed in eight minutes. Will that work?"

"Thanks."

And so, eight minutes later, Joe found himself walking out of the apartment house with Kate as the doorman who was on duty till 8 a.m. tried to avoid smiling at the situation. Joe found himself wondering what she had to do, which was so secretive that she couldn't share. But they'd only known each for other five days.

Joe kissed Kate on the cheek as she got into the Tesla Uber and drove off.

Why didn't I want to tell Joe where I'm going? Kate thought to herself. It would have been so easy to tell him the truth instead of letting him wonder what secret she was hiding. Even though they made love and it was magical, sharing something so important to Kate so soon made her afraid that he might react the wrong way to it. Or maybe she withheld more details because by sharing something so personal and intimate, if he didn't react the right way, it could ruin the beautiful relationship they seemed to be building.

Joe thought of following Kate's Uber to see where she was going but if she saw him, she might think he was stalking her. No, he had to trust that she would share her destination when it was comfortable for her to do so. Boundaries. Healthy boundaries. That's what they needed if they were to make it as a couple. Maybe she was going to meet up with that man, Jennings, she'd been seeing. The one that couldn't make a commitment. Maybe Kate was using him to make that guy jealous? No! She didn't seem the type, Joe reassured himself.

It was hard for Joe to trust so soon after his breakup with Rosemary. He had hoped he learned a thing or two from that relationship and that he could see the red flags sooner, but maybe he had misjudged Kate. Maybe she was going to hurt him even more than Rosemary hurt him.

No, Joe thought to himself. *I've got to give her the benefit of the doubt if this is going to work. I'll find out where Kate went in due course, when she's ready.*

Chapter 7

Kate arrived at Metropolitan Hospital at 6:45 a.m., just fifteen minutes after the scheduled start time that she had committed every Saturday for the last three years. As busy as Kate was with her time management and crime consulting practices and her college teaching, making time to volunteer in the wing for critically ill children was a priority she had never missed. Not even making phenomenal love with Joe as she could tell he was looking forward to a "day-after" day together could stop Kate from coming through for the children who depended on her each week.

It was one way that Kate could better handle the tragic death of her younger cousin Jerome when he was twelve and she was seventeen. It hit Kate hard when he died from his head injuries after the fall from his bicycle. Since Jerome died soon after his fall, he didn't have to spend hours, days, or longer in the hospital like so many of these children that Kate visited. But knowing that some of these children had no one to visit them, especially around the holidays, tugged at Kate's heart.

Most of the time Kate visited just as herself. But other times, she would dress up like a clown, even putting on clown makeup, or put on a funny clown hat for the visits, and she would juggle balls and sing silly songs with the children. Sometimes she'd do facepainting with the kids or make balloon animals. (They had given her a one-hour training in how to make those balloon animals when she started volunteering three years before.)

And it wasn't a short, one-hour visit, either. She would report to the office of the pediatric physician in charge for the day at 7 a.m. There she would be briefed about any children who had special requests or situations. Afterwards she would go from room to room, talking to the children, reading books, singing songs, or doing any of the other clown-related activities. She used her smartphone to play the special playlist she put together for the children, ranging in age from two to fourteen.

For the real little ones, Kate began her visits by singing the timeless, upbeat, "You Are My Sunshine." Those who were dealing with cancer and hoping for remission loved it when she sang "Let It Go" from the movie *Frozen.*

The older children, ages six to ten, especially enjoyed "Happy" by Pharrell Williams. If they were feeling well enough, many would dance with Kate.

And of course, there was always "Here Comes the Sun" by the Beatles, and "You'll Be in My Heart" by Phil Collins from the movie, *Tarzan,* that Kate knew was a hospital playlist favorite.

Today, three hours after she arrived, Kate had made all her rounds. She went to the dressing room for the clown volunteers, removed her makeup, and headed back to her apartment. She thought of calling Joe and seeing if he wanted to come over so they could pick up where they left off that morning, but she was exhausted. She knew she had to pace herself to keep volunteering at the hospital.

These three years of volunteering had been the highlight of her time in New York City since earning her graduate degree from Penn State. But she was emotionally spent. It was hard not to feel anger at the unfairness of it all. That some children were dealt a bad hand. They had an inherited disease, or they picked up something from another child, or they got sick and no one really knew why.

"Why?" was always the question Kate asked as she left the hospital, happy that she, her sister, and her unborn niece all were healthy, as were her parents, relatively young in their sixties. These children, strangers when she first started, had become something between family and friends.

“Special people” is what Kate liked to call them. Very special people.

Intellectually, Kate knew that feeling guilty for her own family’s health was pointless. She wasn’t ready to share this very sacred and special part of her weekly routine with Joe. Not just yet. But hopefully she would be able to, soon. Even though she was tired, as she lay down on her bed to take a short nap, she felt good all over, knowing that she could tell Joe what she did every Saturday, when the time was right. Her gut told her he would appreciate why she ws doing it.

***

Joe and Dennis walked along the row of singles bars, barely noticing the chilly mid-40s temperatures.

“I think flight attendants hang out at this bar,” said Dennis. “Why don’t we go in there and see if we can drum up a conversation?”

“You don’t understand, Dennis. I told you I love this girl.”

“But you also told me that she went off this morning, at 6:30 a.m., somewhere, you don’t know where, and even though you made love last night, she didn’t trust you enough to tell you where she was going.”

"I'm sure she had a good reason."

"That's your problem, Joe," said Dennis. "You're always making excuses for everyone. You made so many excuses for Rosemary. I told you I didn't trust her. That she didn't look at you the way she should have looked at you if she was really in love with you, but you didn't believe me. And look at what happened in the end."

"Please stop bringing up Rosemary. I want to forget her."

"Now that I think of it. Did you get all your things out of her apartment finally?"

"She made sure of that."

"Here's my suggestion," said Dennis. "Get back in the saddle again. The sooner, the better."

"Dennis, I already have. I want Kate."

"Do I have to warn you again? A woman with secrets?"

"Okay. If it will make you feel better, and shut you up about having misgivings about Kate, I'm going to call and ask her about this morning."

"Joe, you'll be making an ass of yourself."

"No, Dennis, I've already made an ass of myself, but I actually don't mind."

"In that case, you might as well call."

"Thanks for understanding. I'll just find a quiet place where I can call her."

"I'll meet you inside. Maybe I'll get lucky," said Dennis.

"It's a plan."

Dennis went into the singles bar as Joe found a quiet place with a bench on a nearby side street.

Kate picked up on the first ring.

"Oh, Kate, it's you. I thought it would go to voice mail."

"No. I'm home."

"Back already?"

"Yes. I just needed three hours to do what I had to do."

"About that…."

"I know it sounded ridiculous and mysterious that I went off like that and I'm sorry that I wouldn't tell you where."

"You're right. Maybe you do really work for the CIA or the FBI after all? Who am I to judge?"

"You're funny," Kate said, trying to make the conversation less awkward than it already was.

"So., Do I have to beg, or will you fill me in?"

"Okay. Here goes. For the last three years, I've been volunteering at a hospital in the critical care children's unit. Sometimes I read them stories, and sometimes I dress up like a clown and entertain them by juggling and doing other silly things."

Joe was speechless.

"Joe, are you still there?"

He took a deep breath.

"Kate, I can't tell you all the things that went through my mind that were the reason you had to run off at 6:30 in the morning and couldn't tell me."

"I'm so sorry but this is a very sacred and special commitment for me. I was afraid of how you would react. I didn't want your reaction to spoil what had been a magical and wonderful evening."

"I'm a little disappointed that you thought I would say something insensitive that wouldn't make you feel good about this amazing and very important way you spend your time. You're my hero, I mean you're my heroine, Kate."

"See. I didn't want you to see me as someone who should be praised or congratulated for doing this. It's hard to explain. I do it because it feels good and right. I think I told you about my first cousin who died of a brain aneurysm when he was twelve and I was seventeen. Even though we were five years apart, we were very close. We liked to hang out with each other. I know he didn't spend a lot of time in the hospital because he died not long after his bicycle accident. But that led me to think about what if he had lived, even for a few days or weeks. What would have made his time in the hospital better."

After a few moments of silence, Joe said, "Thanks for letting me know, Kate."

"Here's another thing I'm going to share with you."

"I'm all ears."

"You're the only one who knows I do this besides my best friend, Brenda. My own sister doesn't know. My parents. No one at the college where I teach. No one else. You're part of a very small circle of people I trust with my secret."

"I'm honored, Kate."

"Thank you for saying that!"

There was another brief silence.

"What are you doing now?" Kate asked.

"Hanging out with my friend Dennis, the one who sorta introduced us. Why?"

"Would you like to come over?"

"Don't you have more dates lined up?"

"I'm actually free for the rest of the day."

"Okay. I can be there in thirty minutes."

"Sounds good."

"I'll go tell Dennis he's on his own! I'm sure he won't mind."

Joe hurried back to the bar. Inside he found Dennis talking to two flight attendants.

"Dennis, I have to go."

Dennis nodded to his audience. "Excuse me a moment, ladies." He led Joe toward the bar.

"Now, what's going on? Where are you going? I was just telling those two lovely women that—"

"Kate invited me to her apartment."

"Kate? Did you find out why she bolted this morning?"

"Yes."

"And…"

"I can't tell you?"

"Why not? I'm your best friend. We don't have any secrets."

"Kate asked me not to."

There was a distinct silence after Joe's declaration.

Dennis quickly reflected back on their decades-long friendship. This was a scenario he was used to by now. They'd get close as two single men and then one or both would meet a woman and become a couple. The secrets would start. The change in the when-and-where they could get together. It was happening again and Dennis knew there was nothing he could do to stop it. He would just have to let Joe playthings out with Kate as he had played it out with Rosemary and so many previous girlfriends.

"No problem, Joe. I'll catch you later."

"Thanks for understanding, Dennis."

"As the saying goes, 'That's what friends are for.'"

Chapter 8

“Coffee, black, two artificial sweeteners,” Kate said as she put the coffee cup next to Joe’s side of the bed.

She kissed Joe on the cheek.

“Another wonderful night together,” said Joe. “I feel like I should pinch myself.”

“Don’t do that!”

At that moment, Kate’s downstairs buzzer went off.

“Who’s that?” Joe asked.

“I don’t know.”

“Are you going to find out?”

“Yes. Sure.”

Kate went to the front door where the intercom was located.

“Who’s there?”

“It’s Bob.”

Kate could feel her whole body tensing. *Bob,* she said to herself. Yes, Bob. He was her date for lunch today.

"Yes, Bob. Sorry. I forgot."

"Do you want to cancel?"

"No. That's all right. Can you give me some time to get ready?"

"How long do you need?"

"Ten, at the most fifteen minutes."

"Sure."

"There's a Starbucks on the corner. They usually have available seats. I'll meet you there in fifteen minutes."

"Sounds like a plan."

Kate went into her bedroom.

"Sorry, Joe, but you have to get dressed. I have a date in fifteen minutes at Starbucks."

"A date?"

"Yes. I told you I'm not going to stop dating till I have a lifelong commitment from Mr. Right."

"Can I ask you an insensitive question?" When she nodded, he said, "Are you planning to sleep with him, too?"

Kate almost slapped him. But she slammed her hand on the end table next to him instead.

"That was definitely an insensitive thing to say. I can date without sleeping with a guy. I told you it was out of character for me to sleep with someone on the second date, but it was special with us."

"*Was* special?"

"*Is* special!"

"Okay. Thanks for the reassurance," said Joe.

"So, we're okay now? You understand the situation? Remember I'm a woman on a mission. I am looking for Mr. Right. I want to find him and to live with him. I want us to start a family before it's too late. I'm turning thirty-nine tomorrow. The clock is ticking."

"I understand. But we only met on December first. I need more time."

"Like Jennings? You need another year?"

"I don't know how long I need. I just know I need more than a week! Can't you give me that?"

"I can try, but no exclusivity until I get a ring."

Kate's confused feelings about Jennings, who was on pause, flashed through her mind. She also wondered if she was letting herself get too close to Joe too soon.

"Copy that," Joe replied as he rolled out of bed and got dressed.

He took another few sips of coffee. As he was leaving, he said to Kate, "You win. I'll call you."

***

The date with Bob was only a four out of ten if she had to give him a rating. Nothing like 9.5 out of 10 that she had ranked Joe Wexler.

Joe hadn't called yet and Kate decided it was best to let everything that happened last night and today sink in before calling him. She knew it was a lot to ask a man she was having an intimate relationship with to "let her" date other men even though she reassured Joe she would not sleep with anyone else.

She knew that was an unconventional approach. Men wanted exclusivity even if they didn't make the full commitment. That's what Jennings had asked of her for the last two years. Jennings. She couldn't believe that, in her mind at least, they were still technically a couple.

Kate decided to go to her shared office space where she met clients for her consulting practice. It was more professional and granted her more privacy than meeting anyone in her apartment. The office space was nice with huge windows overlooking the Hudson River. It was a trek from her apartment, but she usually liked the walk. It had become her three- or four-times per week exercise routine. The other day, she got on MetroNorth to the college in Westchester where she taught in-person once a week. The rest of the week she taught remotely.

When she reached the office, Kate let herself in and got busy with paperwork at her desk.

The door creaked open and Kate looked up.

"Brenda!" Kate said, surprised. "What are you doing here?"

"I knew you weren't in your apartment, it's a non-teaching day, and if you weren't with that new guy, what's his name, Joe, I figured you were here."

"And you're right!" said Kate. "You know me so well."

Brenda handed Kate a box, gift wrapped.

"What's this?"

"A birthday present."

"But my birthday's not till tomorrow!" Kate replied.

'Yeah, but I figured you'd be spending it with Jennings or Joe or some other guy whose name starts with J.

"Ha, ha. That's very funny."

"Well, aren't you going to open it?" Brenda asked.

"Sure."

Kate opened the box and took out a beautiful turquoise sweater.

"Turquoise. My favorite color," Kate said.

"And it's also your birthstone!"

"That's right. Thanks, Brenda." Kate's phone pinged, and she glanced at it. "Oh, it's Jennings texting me."

Brenda tried to peek at Kate's phone. "So, what are you and Jennings going to do for your birthday?"

Kate frowned, then shrugged and put down her phone. "So, it seems we're actually not getting together. His text says he has a bad cold, and he doesn't want to give it to me so he's sorry, but he can't get together with me tomorrow."

"Oh no. That sucks. Will you tell Joe?"

"I don't know. I don't want Joe to think I'm desperate."

"I have an idea," said Brenda. "Let's pick up some chicken soup and go visit Jennings. That could be just what he needs to get over his cold."

"He likes chicken. Sure. Why not?"

Kate and Brenda stopped at the local health food store that was known for its homemade soups.

"Chicken soup is one of our bestsellers," said the clerk.

"Thanks so much. Can you include a plastic soup spoon with that? And maybe some crackers?"

"Sure. Coming right up."

***

"I don't want any romantic advice," Kate said as they rode the subway together, holding the container of chicken soup in an insulated tote.

"I've known you too long to try to give you any. Besides, look at me! I can't talk. I'm still single and I don't have a Jennings or a Joe in my life right now."

“Don’t put yourself down, Brenda. You have a lot going for you. You don’t give yourself enough credit.”

“You’re right about that.”

“We’re here,” said Kate as they got off at the 50th Street subway stops. It was one of Kate’s favorites because of the lovely mosaic tiling added to it years before. It was the stop that tourists often used because it was near some of the Broadway shows.

“Just two blocks up to Jennings’s apartment house.”

“Glad it’s not that cold today,” Brenda replied.

Several tenants were going into the building at the same time, so Brenda and Kate joined them in the elevator. They rode to the penthouse floor, where Jennings had his spacious apartment.

Kate rang the doorbell.

“Coming,” said a woman’s voice.

“That’s not good,” said Brenda, “unless he has a maid.”

A woman wearing a man’s shirt answered the door. She didn’t have any pants on, and the shirt was open revealing a lovely red lace bra.

"Jennings, it must be the pizza delivery," the woman said.

Jennings came to the door.

"Please go back into the bedroom," Jennings said to the woman. "It's not the pizza delivery."

"So, who is it?" the woman asked.

"I'll explain later."

There was silence as the woman cast angry looks at Kate and Brenda before retreating.

"I'm going back downstairs," said Brenda. "Kate, I'll see you down there. You going to be all right?"

"I'll be fine. This won't take long."

"Kate. What are you doing here?" Jennings asked.

"You texted that you had a cold and that's why you can't go out with me for my birthday tomorrow. I felt sorry for you, so I brought you some homemade chicken soup from my favorite health food store.

"Okay, I can see that. But you came over without calling first?"

"You mean calling first to warn you so you could ask whatever bimbo it is that you're shacking up with to get out so I wouldn't know?"

"She's no bimbo, Kate. She happens to be a neurologist at Mt. Sinai Hospital."

"I don't care if she's an astronaut with NASA. I thought we were still 'a thing.'"

"'A thing'" repeated Jennings. "What are you talking about? You agreed to our 'pause.'"

"I must be crazy to still want to be with you, but a side of me thought we still had a chance, as a couple. Or maybe it's just because I got used to us being together. It's been two years."

"But you keep pressuring me to go to 'the next step.' I do care about you, Kate. But I'm not ready."

"I don't think we should get into this now," said Kate.

"Agreed."

Kate turned to go back downstairs.

"Oh, I forgot. Here's your chicken soup."

She gave him the chicken soup although she now wondered if he even had a cold.

***

Bzzz. Bzzz. Bzzz.

Who's buzzing like that? wondered Joe.

Bzzz. Bzzz. Bzzz.

"I'm coming," he said in a loud voice.

Joe looked through the peep hole in Dennis' front door. It was Kate.

"Kate! How'd you find me? I don't think I ever gave you my address?"

"No, but Dennis did when we first met, to convince me you two were 'safe'. I put it in my contacts."

"What are you doing here? Are you all right?"

"Not really."

"Why don't you come in and tell me all about it."

"Okay, but it relates to guys. Will that be awkward?"

"Yes, but that's okay."

Kate walked into Dennis' apartment. She glanced at the sofa that was still an unmade sofa bed in the middle of the living room.

Joe removed the pillows and the blanket, folding up the sofa bed and turning his makeshift bed back into the living room.

"Don't worry about that," Kate said. "I need to talk to someone who cares."

"That's definitely me."

"Okay. So, I thought I'd be spending my birthday with that guy I told you about. Jennings. Even though we're technically on 'pause' we had agreed ages ago that we'd be together for my birthday and it's tomorrow. But he texted that he had a cold, so my friend Brenda had the bright idea to get him chicken soup for his cold and go over to his apartment and give it to him. But when we did that, a woman answered. She was wearing a man's shirt. It must be some woman he's sleeping with."

"Oh boy!"

"So, I left and then, on top of that, I immediately called my parents and asked them to get together. But they turned me down because they said we got together recently for that family wedding. They want to space out our visits."

"I can't believe they said that."

Kate started crying, very softly.

"Joe, I don't want to spend my birthday alone. And I don't want to spend it with Brenda, either. Yes, she's my best friend but she can be a downer sometimes."

"So, what about me? I'd love to spend your birthday with you!"

"You would?"

"Absolutely!"

There was a brief pause as Kate considered what Joe had just said.

"Okay. So, what will we do for my birthday?"

"Leave that to me," Joe answered. "It will be a surprise."

"Okay."

"Do you want to stay here tonight?" asked Joe.

"If it's okay with you, I want to go back to my apartment and have a good cry. Then I'll be ready to spend my birthday with you tomorrow."

"And don't forget to look at how many birthday wishes you get on your Facebook timeline tomorrow," Joe suggested.

"You think I should do that? One of my friends got sixty birthday wishes. Another got one hundred-twenty-five! One hundred-twenty-five people wished her a happy birthday on her Facebook timeline. What if I only get ten or twenty?"

"Don't worry about how many you get. We'll be together. Those Facebook timeline wishes are gravy."

"Good point."

"See you tomorrow. I'll pick you up at eleven if that's okay."

"Sounds terrific!"

***

Joe started by making a lunch reservation at the Italian restaurant Kate said was her favorite in the theater district. They had checkered tablecloths which was important to him and he had viewed the menu online and saw there were plenty of vegetarian options. They thoughtfully made a point of noting that the minestrone soup was made with vegetable stock, not beef stock.

After that, he made some phone calls and managed to get two Orchestra seats to a show that Kate had mentioned she'd like to see. It was going to cost him a couple of hundred dollars but she was worth it. Besides, the robot wife he invented that his company was manufacturing was going to start selling by January first.

Where should he take her afterwards? Joe wondered. The show would be over by ten o'clock. Too early to go back to her apartment on her birthday night. What about that piano bar in that hotel on 42nd Street that he always liked to go to when he needed to get out at night? He checked online and his favorite singer was still performing there. Tickets were available for the second show, which started at eleven p.m. for the late-night crowd.

He purchased two tickets online, downloading the confirmation to his smartphone.

Now, the next most crucial decision regarding Kate's birthday. What should he get her for a present?

Jewelry is permanent and always appreciated, but he instinctively felt it was a bit too soon in their romance for that. What about a sweater? No, Kate told him Brenda got her a sweater. He wanted to stay out of the friend zone on that.

Before music went pretty much all online, he could have bought her a CD of one of her favorite singers, like Lady Gaga or Adele. But everything was downloaded now. Giving her a gift card so she could do music downloads was just too tacky for a romantic gift.

A book. Yes, that would be the perfect gift. Something tangible. He could get her a book by one of his favorite authors. There were so many. Elmore Leonard. Nelson DeMille. He loved reading mysteries. He hesitated to get her an Elmore Leonard novel since most of those had only male protagonists. The female characters were never as strong or as pivotal in the novels.

Nelson DeMille's *The Gold Coast* was often praised as his best work. Joe also thought of getting a second book. Yes, this was an obvious choice in terms of how he had grown to feel about Kate, the love that was growing within him every moment, every day. It had to be *Sonnets from the Portuguese* by Elizabeth Barrett Browning. So powerful and so meaningful to include a collection of poems published in 1850 but still timeless. Who does not remember one of the most famous lines of love poetry ever written? "How do I love thee? Let me count the ways..."

***

Joe's plans worked. Every minute of the next day was thrilling for both Kate and Joe. The restaurant choice was perfect. The play was funny and upbeat. There were even a couple of memorable songs in it, a necessity for Kate who always judged musicals by the plot and the characters but also by how many memorable songs she hummed as she exited the theater.

The evening performance was outstanding. Bravo that the singer, at age ninety-two, was still belting out those love songs as if she was fifty-two. She got a standing ovation and deservedly so.

The two books that Joe lovingly wrapped himself and gave to Kate were well-received.

He had inscribed both to her personally. In the Nelson DeMille novel he wrote, “A woman of mystery whom I have grown to love,” and he signed it, “Love always, Joe.”

In the poetry collection he wrote, “I can’t count the ways I love you yet because there are too many to count! With love, Joe.”

Their lovemaking was even more pleasurable and mutually exciting and satisfying than the previous two times they had consummated their connection.

“This was the best birthday ever,” Kate declared the next morning.

“Ever?” repeated Joe.

“This one beat my Sweet Sixteen. It’s definitely my favorite birthday now! Thanks, Joe, for your thoughtfulness. Everything was great. Lunch. The show. The performer. The presents…." She kissed him. "And everything else."

"What shall we do on the first day of your thirty-ninth year?"

"Wow! Thirty-nine. That sounds so old."

"Not at all! You're beautiful, successful, amazing. So. How about a run?"

"Okay. Let's do it."

Kate got into her running shoes. It was cold but the snow had melted over the last few days. There was a run/walk path along the East River that they could use.

After their run, as they strolled back to Kate's apartment, hand-in-hand, Kate said to Joe, "How do you feel about marriage?"

"Marriage," Joe replied. "It's a wonderful institution. I believe in it one hundred percent."

"So, how would you feel about marrying me?"

"You?"

"Yes, me," Kate replied matter-of-factly.

Joe stopped walking and put his hands gently on Kate's shoulders. But before he could answer, Kate blurted, "Forget it."

She took off running toward her apartment.

"No, wait!" Joe caught up with her.

"I said forget it."

"But can't we talk about this?" Joe asked.

"It was actually a hypothetical question."

"Look," Joe said. "Here's the deal. I've seen you go outside the apartment to get a cigarette. I know you smoke. It's nothing to be ashamed of. We all have habits that we know aren't healthy. It's just that I could never marry a woman who smoked. It's not just because of me, I'm saying that. It's also because we know passive smoke is harmful to everyone, including any children in the house. And I also wouldn't want to risk losing the woman I married sooner because of smoking."

Kate listened to Joe's every word. She had tried to keep her pack a day habit a secret. She wasn't proud that she smoked. But she hadn't been able to quit since she started smoking a few years ago as a stress reliever. Soon she found herself addicted.

After an uncomfortable silence, she said, "It really was a hypothetical question. I have to go. It was a great date yesterday and last night. Thanks again for my birthday celebration. Give me a call sometime."

With that, Kate took off down the rest of the street in a flash. Joe tried not to look too stunned, but his jaw had definitely dropped. He was confused as he tried replaying what had just happened.

Did I hear her right? he asked himself.

Maybe she *was* asking him about marriage, only hypothetically?

Or not?

Chapter 9

The next day, Joe and Dennis sat in a coffee shop on Bleeker Street in the West Village in a booth by the window. Joe gazed outside, distracted.

Dennis stirred his coffee. "So just like that. She asked you to marry her?"

"Yes," Joe said, turning to his friend. "But then she took it back."

"That's weird. How'd she do that?"

"She said that she was just asking me about marriage, hypothetically."

"Well, at least she didn't punch you. I heard that when Bill Jones asked his girlfriend to marry him, she punched him.

"No, Kate didn't punch me." Joe thought for a moment. "So, what happened with Bill Jones? I don't remember the end to that story?"

"You mean the *punchline*?"

"Ha, ha, ha!"

"They got married. Six years and three kids."

"That's a happy ending."

"For Bill Jones. But every story, every romance, is different. What worked for them may not work for you, or for you and Kate, if Kate turns out to be 'the one.'"

"What am I going to do?" Joe asked Dennis.

"Do you love her?"

"Yes, I do love her. But marriage? It just seems…"

"A little soon," said Dennis.

"Exactly. After all, we've only known each other a couple of weeks."

"That's right! But you did tell me she's a time management consultant. Maybe she has a keener sense of time than most people."

"That's possible. Except that, this morning, she's talking about marriage. Then this afternoon, she's on three more dates with guys from three different dating apps."

"How'd you find that out?" asked Dennis.

"She friended me on Facebook and she's reporting her dating activities to everyone in her friend circle. I think she's up to number forty-three since she started her 'search for Mr. Right' campaign."

"So that means you were—what, her thirtieth date?"

"Something like that."

"How long has her 'campaign' been going on?"

"Technically all her life but realistically since her sister told her that she was pregnant. I think that was about a month ago."

"Wow. Forty-three dates in just a month or so. It's astonishing she's had time to do anything else."

"That's probably where those time management skills come in handy. Except that she does tend to be late most of the time."

"The cobbler whose kids go without shoes syndrome?"

"Something like that," said Joe, "but let's not say anything disparaging about—"

"Your girlfriend?" Dennis chimed in.

"She's not my girlfriend yet."

"But you said you're in love with her?"

"Yes, I am."

"Let's get back to the Bill Jones example. When he proposed to his future wife and she punched him. And I want to add that she never punched him again. She's not an abusive person."

"So, what are you telling me?" asked Joe.

"Some people don't want to be pressured. It can make them do terrible things," said Dennis.

"Like punching someone."

"Exactly," said Dennis.

"So, I don't want to be pressured?" Joe asked.

"That's right. And it's okay to feel that way, Joe. They say the two biggest decisions we make as adults are what we're going to do for a career, and who we marry.

"You're right about that!"

They sipped their coffees. Then Joe said, "Thanks, Dennis. But can we switch the topic for a moment too?

"Work! I thought you'd never ask," said Dennis. "I am pleased to report that we have twenty orders for our robot wife."

"If my math is correct, that's four-hundred-thousand dollars!" Joe exclaimed.

"Yes, but that's not the net. First, we have to cover costs for manufacturing, program development, factory overhead like rent, and salaries including the fee plus royalties we agreed to pay Rosemary for being our prototype," Dennis said. "That gives us a net of around seventy-five thousand."

"Does that include our salaries?"

"We don't earn a *salary,* Joe. We're investors and inventors, so we get a percentage of the profits."

Joe nodded. "After all is said and done, what can you and I expect to take in during the month of January for the last two years of our life's work?"

"I think we can squeeze out ten thousand to each of us."

Joe sat quietly for a moment. Then he said, "That's something."

"Yes, that's something."

"But it's not a million dollars," Joe added.

"No, it's not a million. But it's something."

Joe pushed his cup away, and sighed. "This is a very depressing way to end our conversation, Dennis. I think I'm going to go now. I have to digest what you've just told me. I also think I'll have to stay on your couch a while longer."

"Stay as long as you want to, need to, my friend."

***

Joe asked Kate's doorman to let her know he was there. Her building had a doorman from four p.m. everyday till eight the next morning. It was forty-thirty.

"She said you can go up."

Joe didn't have to knock on Kate's door. She was standing there, with the door ajar.

"This is a pleasant surprise," Kate said.

"We have to talk," Joe said.

"Okay. Come in."

"You're alone?" Joe asked.

"That's a rude thing to say. I wouldn't have invited you in if there was someone here."

"You're right. Sorry. I didn't mean to be rude. But you shared on Facebook that you do have more dates lined up for today.

"Okay. What do you want to talk about?" Kate asked.

"Are you kidding? I know it's been twenty-four hours since our run and since your proposal…"

"Wait a minute. You know I told you it was a *hypothetical* question."

"Come on, Kate. Initially you did ask me to marry you."

"Please don't embarrass me or yourself."

"Okay. I certainly don't want that."

"Joe, before you say anything else, I want to let you know that I quit smoking this morning."

"Just like that?"

"Just like that. I put my last cigarette in a yogurt container."

"I'm happy for you," Joe replied. "Good for you."

"Sorry I interrupted you," said Kate. "So. What do you want, Joe Wexler?"

"I want you to stop seeing other men."

"Hmmm. Is that a proposal?"

"A proposal?"

"You said you didn't want me seeing other men. So, are you proposing marriage?"

Before Joe could reply, Kate got a call on her cell phone.

"Sorry, Joe, I have to take this."

She could tell it was Jennings from caller ID.

Kate went into the bedroom and closed the door to take the call.

"Hi, Kate. It's Jennings."

"I know."

"Listen. I want to apologize about the other day and about your birthday. What a mess! So sorry this all happened."

"What's up, Jennings?"

"Aren't you hearing me? I'm apologizing."

"That's nice of you."

"Listen, I'm going to Dallas on a short business trip, but I'd like to take you out to dinner and start over, stop the pause, when I get back. I really care for you, and I want to build on the two years we've spent together."

Kate was upset with herself as she realized she was still susceptible to Jennings's selfish but enthralling way of manipulating her. What was it about that man? His looks? His impressive pedigree?

His flashy apartment and the expensive restaurants? They hadn't had sex in the weeks since they stopped actively seeing each other, but she had to admit, it was always pleasant enough when they did.

There was a long silence. Jennings jumped in to stop the uncomfortable quiet.

"Listen, you don't have to decide now. I know what happened the other day was embarrassing and downright humiliating to you. Will you at least let me call you when I get back from Dallas, and we can see about that dinner?"

Kate hesitated before deciding she had nothing to lose to at least let him call her when he returned.

"Sure. Give me a call then, and we'll see where we stand at that point. I have to get back to my company now."

"Understood."

"Have a good trip," Kate added.

"Take care. And a belated happy birthday."

"Thanks."

When Kate returned to the living room, she found Joe sitting in her oversized reading chair in the corner of the room. He was scrolling through his phone to distract himself until Kate returned.

"May I ask what was so important that you had to take the call? We were in the midst of a very key discussion about our relationship!"

"Please don't get controlling on me. I can't take controlling men!"

"I'm not being controlling. I'm just curious!" said Joe, his voice louder but not shouting.

"And you're being very nosy. Well, if you have to know, it was Jennings."

"Your ex?"

"My sorta ex."

"So, he's still in your life even after what happened the other day?"

"He told me it was all a horrible misunderstanding and an error in judgment on his part."

"Nothing you've told me about this guy makes me think that he'd be the right man for you to spend your life with."

"My mother likes him."

"Your mother?"

Kate shook her head. "You're right, what does my mother have to do with anything!"

"Let's get back to our discussion. Why can't we just date, and see what happens?" asked Joe.

"I've said this before, Joe, but I'll say it again. I've just turned thirty-nine and I want to get married and have a family. The clock is ticking."

"But we hardly know each other."

"What more do you need to know about me? I know enough about you to give it a try."

"There are still things to get to know."

"It's a moot point. I asked you to marry me, and you said no. On to the next, as they say."

"I didn't say no. I said I needed more time." Joe thought for a moment and then he added, "Look, you mentioned your mother. So maybe it's time that I meet your mother. And your father, too."

"Great idea. My sister Melanie and her husband Jerry can join us as well."

"Yes. I'd really like to meet your family."

"And I'd like to meet yours!"

Chapter 10

Two days later, on Christmas Day, the entire Hellman clan, including Kate's sister Melanie and her husband Jerry were sitting at a round table in the Palm Court at the Plaza Hotel. It was easier for everyone if they all met at the Plaza since Melanie and Jerry would be driving in from their home in Silver Spring, Maryland and Kate's parents would be driving from downtown Philadelphia, in Rittenhouse Square, officially called Center City, where Kate grew up. The elder Hellmans had downsized from a townhouse to a condo since her father sold his medical practice and retired.

"I'm pleased to meet you, Mrs. Hellman. Mr. Hellman. —I mean, Doctor Hellman! Kate has told me so much about both of you," said Joe.

"Is that true or is that something you say?" Mrs. Hellman replied.

Joe, taken back a bit, jumped right in with, "And it's nice to meet you, Melissa, I mean, Melanie, and your husband, Jerry."

"Yes, we're Melanie and Jerry."

"Sorry," Joe said. "I'm nervous."

"Don't be so nervous. We're just Kate's family."

"You're right," Joe replied.

"Let's eat," said Doctor Hellman. "I'm starving."

"Relax, Dad," said Kate. "We'll get food soon."

At this time of year, the restaurant was crowded. It was one of the top places for brunch in Manhattan, especially during the holiday season. It was also one of the few restaurants open on Christmas Day. What a festive scene to see the natural evergreen tree, almost touching the ceiling, decorated with tiny white lights in the Plaza's lobby.

On the opposite side of the room was an oversized menorah, with three electric lights lit up commemorating that today was the fourth day of Hanukah. The fourth electric candle would be turned on at sundown.

Kate sat next to Joe. On Joe's other side was Kate's father.

"I'm so sorry I called you 'Mister' Hellman before," Joe said.

"It's okay. I was a doctor. I'm retired now so you can call me Mister Hellman."

"Kate told me you were also in the war."

"Yes, the Vietnam War. I served two years in the medical corps. Horrible experience. Worst two years of my life. I still have PTSD from it."

"Sorry I brought it up."

"Yes, Joe," said Melanie. "Dad would prefer to avoid talking about the Vietnam War."

"My apologies."

"Switching the subject. Retired. That must be nice."

"It's death," Doctor Hellman quickly replied.

"Does anyone have to go to the little girl's room?" Mrs. Hellman asked.

"Sure," said Kate.

"I can always go," said Melanie as she rubbed her belly, almost five months along now.

Inside the luxurious bathroom, in the oversized lounge area, Mrs. Hellman looked at Kate and said, "How could you bring a total stranger to our family brunch?"

"Mother," Kate began, "I'm dating Joe."

"This is the first I'm hearing about it."

"And I've asked him to marry me," Kate added.

"Well, that's the end of him," replied her stunned mother.

"We'll see."

"And what about Jennings? I really like him," Mrs. Hellman added.

"I know you do, Mother, but he's a commitment phobic."

"What does that mean?"

"It's someone who can't commit to marriage," explained Melanie.

"Maybe he just needs more time."

"That's what he says but I don't believe him anymore," said Kate.

"Okay, dear, but you don't just go around asking men to marry you. That scares them more than anything. You have to let them ask *you*. You have to make them feel it's their idea. That makes them feel in charge," her mother continued.

"Times have changed, Mother," said Kate.

"Not that much. In my day there was that one day a year when a woman could ask a man to marry her. I think it's on February 29th, when there's a leap year."

"So that's only every four years," added Melanie.

"That's too long to wait!," exclaimed Kate. "But you don't have to worry. Joe turned me down. Said he needed more time, so we'll have to see what happens. But I'm not waiting around. I'm still dating men I'm meeting through the dating apps, and I've also had introductions lately through several friends."

"Kate, you are thirty-nine years old. You're not getting any younger. Whether it's Jennings or this one," said Mrs. Hellman. "I was married with three young children by thirty-nine."

"Yes, mother, I know. And my date's name is Joe, mother. Joe."

"Okay, Joe. Try to keep at least one of them from running away."

After an hour, once her parents and her sister Melanie her husband Jerry shared about various streaming series they were all watching, with little else to talk about, it was time to wrap up the Christmas Day breakfast with her parents and sister.

"Sorry we have to run but we promised Joe's parents that we'd spend Christmas Day with them," said Kate as she stood from the table.

"Before you leave, please take your Hanukah present," said Doctor Hellman.

"Don't you think I'm too old for that?" asked Kate.

"Talk for yourself," said Melanie.

"That's right, Kate. Don't answer for your sister," said Mrs. Hellman.

With that, Doctor Hellman took two envelopes from his overcoat pocket.

"Here you go," he said to his daughters as he passed along the envelopes.

"Thanks, Dad," said Melanie.

"Yes, thanks Mom and Dad," Kate added.

"Aren't you going to open it?" asked Mrs. Hellman.

"I'll open it later," Kate answered.

"I'll open mine now, if you like," said Melanie. And four crisp $100 bills fell out from the envelope.

"That's very generous of you both," said Melanie. She started to get up from her chair to kiss her parents, but her mother stopped her.

"No need for all that emotion, Melanie, especially not in your condition. We know you're grateful."

"Thanks again, Mom and Dad," Kate added as she and Joe headed for the exit.

***

Joe and Kate had rented a car for the day. Fortunately, there were still a few compact vehicles left even though it was Christmas. It was hard for Joe to fit inside the car because of his height, but he managed. Luckily, it would only be a two hour and thirty-minute drive to visit his parents in Rotterdam, a town near Schenectady, New York that was considered a suburb.

The morning was behind them. They had survived brunch with Kate's family. Joe picked up the tab, which everyone seemed to appreciate.

Now they were on their way to Rotterdam, New York to visit Joe's parents and at least one of his four siblings. That was one of the many contrasts between Joe and Kate. Kate, with just one sibling, and Joe, from a big family with four siblings, two girls and two boys. Joe was the oldest. Joe, the carnivore and

Kate, the vegetarian. Joe the Christian and Kate, although she didn't go to synagogue and only observed the two high holy days every year, Yom Kippur and Rosh Hashanah, was Jewish. Joe grew up in Rotterdam, in upstate New York, a suburb of around thirty thousand. A stark contrast to where Kate grew up, in Philadelphia, a city with around 1.5 million residents.

Joe had told Kate many times how much his family got into the Christmas spirit. They did the tree decorating, gift exchange, holiday ham meal, singing Christmas carol sing-a-long—the whole nine yards.

"I should probably tell you something about my family to prepare you," said Joe.

"You met mine. How bad could yours be?"

Two hours later, they pulled onto the paved driveway of a quaint, ranch-style home surrounded by Maple, Birch, and Oak trees. In the front of the house was a huge, blow-up oversized Santa Claus. Kate heard that this year there was a shortage of those Santas. Joe explained his dad bought that Santa a few years before. He used an electric pump to inflate it every year. After it was deflated, it was stored in the attic, along with their voluminous Christmas lights.

White lights covered almost every inch of the house, surrounding the windows and going up and down the sides. There were also lights in the trees next to the house. It was still daylight, so the lights were not turned on yet. But the Santa was the focal point of the yard.

Within a few moments of their arrival, Kate and Joe were startled to see a woman in her mid-60s holding a shotgun and using it to tap the window to get their attention.

"Mom," shouted Joe. "Will you put that thing away!"

"Joe? That you? Sorry, son. I just wanted to make sure you weren't robbers coming to tie us up and steal everything we have in the house.

"No, Mom. We're not robbers."

"Welcome, welcome," said Joe's mom, as she put the shotgun down by her side.

"Can you put that thing away, please. It's making me nervous."

"Okay, okay," said Mrs. Wexler.

"Where's Dad?" Joe asked.

"He's either outside or inside. One or the other."

"Okay," Joe replied.

Inside, in the kitchen, was Joe's father, Brendan Wexler, standing six-foot, seven-inches tall. Just two years older than Joe's mother, he was starting to go bald as his hairline was receding. But he still had plenty of dark hair.

"Do you want something to drink?" Mr. Wexler asked Kate.

"I'll take some coffee if you have it."

"I meant a real drink. Whiskey?"

"Dad, Kate doesn't drink."

"Let's all go into the living room and sit down. Dinner won't be ready for another hour or so," Mrs. Wexler said. Even though she was only in her early sixties, her hair was completely white. She didn't wear any makeup. She was wearing a beige sweater over a pair of brown slacks. What a stark contrast to Kate's mother whose hair was still a deep, dark brown. Kate's mother always wore makeup, including false eyelashes, and took pains when appearing in public to be dressed in her finest. This morning, she wore a black satin suit trimmed with real white fur.

"Sure," said Joe.

"You keeping my boy out of trouble down there in New York City?" Mr. Wexler asked Kate. "I don't know what he sees in that place. I don't know why he wants to live there, why he won't come back here where we have trees. And we're only thirty minutes from Schenectady."

"Okay Dad…" said Joe.

"Do you like it down there, Kate?" Mr. Wexler asked.

"It has its good—"

"Don't compare with here, though," Mr. Wexler continued.

"Dad, nothing compares with here," Joe said.

Kate smiled at Joe's sarcasm.

"You couldn't pay me to live down there," said Mr. Wexler.

"I—" Kate began.

"Let me get you a scotch," Mr. Wexler said.

"Get me a small scotch and Kate a coffee, Dad, okay?"

"Want some brandy in your coffee, Kate? Kate, is it?"

"No, thank you. But thank you for asking."

"How about a cigarette?" asked Mr. Wexler. A chain smoker, Joe's father dismissed the health warnings about tobacco.

"Dad, Kate just quit smoking," Joe quickly replied.

"Then she's probably still craving one," said Mr. Wexler.

"No thank you," Kate said, politely, trying to hide her displeasure.

The awkwardness continued for another ten minutes. It only stopped when Joe's younger sister, Greer, arrived with her two children. She and Joe were two years apart.

"Kate, this is Greer. And these are Greer's children, Wayne and Linda. Wayne is seven, and Linda's nine."

"So nice to meet all of you," Kate said.

The next two hours were filled with questions back and forth about Joe's top secret new invention, which of course he had to decline answering, as well as what Kate did for a living and what Greer and her family thought of New York City. They bragged about living in nearby Schenectady although Greer confessed, she secretly always dreamed about renting an apartment in Manhattan for a month or two. She'd go to all the Broadway shows and get tickets to the TV shows that had an audience. Then she'd stand outside some of the morning talk show studios and be part of the audience looking out the windows. Maybe she'd even wave.

"New York," Greer concluded. "That would be a great place to visit…"

"'But I wouldn't want to live there…'is the way that saying goes," said Kate.

"Oh, but I would like to live there," Greer explained. I'd even bring the kids with me. But just for a month or two. Not all the time."

"Thanks, Greer," said Joe. "At least someone in this family understands the appeal and magic of New York City."

"And what is that you do?" Greer asked Kate, switching the subject.

"I teach college courses and I'm also a time management and crime consultant."

"That's quite a range of jobs," Greer remarked.

"Yes it is," Kate agreed.

"What do you teach?"

"Sociology and criminology courses," Kate replied.

“Can you give me an example of a criminology course you teach?”

“One course I teach practically every semester is victimology.”

“What’s that?” asked Mrs. Wexler.

“It’s the scientific study of crime victims,” Kate replied.

“I’ve never heard of that,” Greer added.

“Is that a real thing?” asked Mr. Wexler. “I’ve never heard of studying someone who’s the victim of the crime. I’ve only heard about studying the criminals.”

“Dad, I think the term they use today is offenders, rather than criminals,” said Greer.

“Criminals, Offenders. What’s the difference? The people who did it.”

“Food’s on,” said Joe, eager to switch the subject. He could tell things were getting too intense now.

“Sounds great,” said Kate. “Thanks, by the way, for asking about my teaching, but I know it can get a little heavy at times to hear about it.”

“But it’s fascinating, Kate,” said Greer. “I’ve been working in human resources at a branch office of a computer technology company. I'll finish up my nursing degree and go back to that when the kids are older."

By six o'clock, they had exchanged presents, with Joe especially programmed to act surprised when he received, once again, a sweater he would probably never wear for his gift. Greer included Kate in the gift-giving, which was thoughtful. It was a bath set that she picked up at the department store, with bath salts, soap, and a decorative washcloth. Everything was lavender. Kate immediately knew it was not something she would ever use, but it was the thought that counted.

"Thanks so much, Greer," Kate said, giving her a hug.

"You're very welcome," Greer replied, smiling.

Joe gave out gifts to everyone in his family, not just Greer's children, which impressed Kate. Even if his parents were less than enthusiastic about their Christmas gifts, it was a time-honored tradition that Kate could see everyone thoroughly appreciated. Kate had brought an oversized basket of goodies for the entire family that included wine, cookies, nuts, dried fruits, popcorn, and so much more. It was impressive and festive but now she regretted not getting individual gifts for each of Joe's family members.

But it was finally time to say goodbye since they were not staying overnight. Although Joe grew up in a semi-rural area without too many streetlights at night, so he was used to driving in the dark, he preferred to get on the road sooner than later. Although he had accepted scotch from his father shortly after their arrival, he just did that to placate his father. He knew enough to avoid drinking since he would be driving back to the city.

In just those few, short hours, Kate found herself getting attached to Joe's family. But she was especially taken with Joe's niece and nephew. They were very bright children especially when they could take their eyes off their tablets or their cell phones and interact with their family members.

"My Mom said you're a time management consultant," said Linda. "What do you do?"

"I help people to manage their time better."

"That's a real thing?" asked Wayne.

I can't believe this kid's only seven, thought Kate. She was used to being around college and graduate students, but she didn't have much experience around seven- and nine-year-olds. They were a lot smarter and tuned into the world than she remembered being at that age. Most everyone complains about the negative impact of the Internet or social media, but Kate was also aware of how much information generations were learning at much earlier ages.

"I think we'll take the back roads down to New York," Joe declared as they left with plenty of leftovers in the back seat.

"I know the food may go bad by the time we get home, but I've learned never to turn down my mother's offer of leftovers," Joe explained. "She takes her cooking very seriously. To Mom, food is love so that's why we had to take all that food back with us.

"No problem," said Kate. "That's actually very sweet."

"Yes, it helps offset our arrival and her greeting us with a shotgun."

They both laughed as they got into their car, taking in the bright Christmas lights that glowed in the early darkness. The Wexler house was so ablaze with Christmas decorations it reminded Joe of one of his all-time favorite holiday movies, *National Lampoon's Christmas Vacation*, starring Chevy Chase.

"I love that movie too," said Kate. "Every time I watch it, I crack up at that scene with the squirrel and the Christmas tree."

Joe smiled. Something else they had in common that he could check off in his box of similarities and contrasts between the two of them.

They were soon driving on US 20. Since it was already getting dark, it was hard to see any of the farmland as they drove by. Kate was scrolling through her phone, looking at the messages, she received during her visit with Joe's family. Nothing was time sensitive, so she didn't have to respond to anyone right away.

After around thirty minutes, Joe pulled off the main road and idled the engine. There were no cars around, which was not unusual in that part of upstate New York.

"What's up?" Kate asked.

Joe took a deep breath. He looked Kate straight in the eyes, and he said, "Will you marry me?"

"What?" Kate asked. "Can you repeat that?"

"I said, 'Will you marry me?' I figured we survived both sets of our parents today, and even some other family members, so why not make it official and start our own family?"

Kate started crying.

"Also, I didn't tell you this, but I told myself that if you gave up smoking, if you loved me enough to do that, I would ask you to marry me. Well, Kate Hellman. Your answer?"

"The answer is 'yes.'"

"I'm sorry I don't have a ring yet."

"So, this was spontaneous?"

"Absolutely. It just came over me as I was driving and I said to myself, 'Why not?' Kate and I love each other. Let's give it a try.'"

"You have to promise me one thing," Kate said.

"What's that?"

"Let's get Brenda and Dennis together and tell them both at the same time."

"Sure. But let's do that after we tell our parents."

"And I tell my sister," said Kate.

"Of course."

"And one more thing," said Kate. "Let's not post it on Facebook just yet. I want to tell Jennings first."

"Understood."

Chapter 11

Jennings took Kate's news that she was getting married better than she expected.

"Call me if it doesn't work out," was his response, which Kate thought was both cruel and somewhat flattering. So maybe he really did hope to someday make a commitment.

The month of December was busy for everyone but for Kate and Joe, it would be the month that they met, fell in love, and would be getting married. They decided they'd rather have a reasonable wedding in Dennis's apartment than spend a lot of money on a big affair. Besides, Doctor Hellman was retired and worried about money, Joe's parents had limited resources, and Kate and Joe were just happy to be together. They didn't need a fifty-thousand-dollar wedding.

But Kate did need a dress. Fortunately, she was a sample size, so she and Brenda made plans to visit the bridal gown section in one of the department stores on Fifth Avenue.

Brenda arrived at Kate's apartment early and helped herself to a beer while she waited for Kate.

When Kate emerged from her room, she frowned at her friend's disheveled appearance. "Brenda," said Kate, "can you put down that beer so we can make it to the store before everything closes. I have to get a wedding dress!"

"What'd you say, Kate?"

"I said we have to get out of here so we can go shopping for my wedding dress."

"You're ar'ight," said Brenda, slurring her words.

"Are you okay to do this today?" Kate asked.

"Do what?"

"We're going shopping."

"Right," said Brenda as she slammed the second beer can on to Kate's kitchen/dining room table.

"I'll call an Uber," Kate said.

Kate tried on several dresses. She found one that was her favorite, but even the sample discounted price was $1,200. Reluctantly, she returned it to the rack.

"That's just out of my budget, even with the three hundred in cash from my parents for Hanukah."

"I thought you said your sister got four hundred from your parents," Brenda commented.

"You're right. I figure the extra hundred is for Melanie's baby. I'm not upset about that. But I'm maxed out on my credit cards. Assistant professors don't make all that much money after I pay the rent on my apartment and my outside office, as well as the weekly commute on Metro North. I'd rather not have to ask Joe to chip in."

"Try it on again," said Brenda. "I'll help you in the dressing room. I didn't really get a good look at it the first time."

"Okay," said Kate.

Once in the dressing room, Brenda helped ease the elegant ivory bridal gown—soft lace, fitted bodice, and all—over Kate's head. Eager to help—and slightly inebriated—Brenda yanked on the dress, inadvertently tearing the sample bridal gown her friend had her heart set on.

"Oops!" said Brenda.

"What's wrong?" Kate asked.

"Oops!" Brenda repeated.

"Brenda, tell me what's wrong."

"I think I tore your dress."

"Oh no!"

"So sorry!" Brenda said, slurring her words. "Now take off your dress and don't say a word about what happened!"

"Why?"

"Trust me," Brenda said.

"Okay. I'm trying."

Kate removed the wedding gown, and Brenda brought it to the check-out counter while Kate got dressed.

"My friend is getting married this Sunday and she wants to buy this dress," Brenda said to the clerk.

"Wow, that's wonderful" said the clerk as she smoothed the dress and looked for the price tag. "Most of the brides I meet are excited about their wedding a few weeks or even a few months away."

The clerk was looking for the price tag on the dress to start ringing up the order. "Oh no," said the horrified clerk. "Unfortunately, there seems to be a tear in the armhole. I'm so sorry about that. But sometimes this happens with the floor samples."

"Oh, no," said Brenda. "My friend has her heart set on this particular dress."

"I'm so very sorry about this! Let me at least see if we can offer your friend a discount. I hope that will be acceptable to her because there isn't enough time to get the dress to our seamstress to repair it before Sunday."

A few minutes later, Kate joined them at the counter, and the clerk repeated her offer.

"That's very gracious of you," said Kate as Brenda discreetly winked at her.

"I just have to talk to my manager. I am so sorry this happened."

"Okay. We'll wait."

About five minutes later, the clerk returned.

"My manager apologized profusely and he said we could discount the dress to nine hundred."

"Okay."

"Can I go to the ATM and bring back the cash?" Kate asked.

"Sure. I'll put the dress aside for you."

"Let me know what the total will be including tax."

The clerk used a calculator next to the register. She wrote it down on a piece of paper and slipped it to Kate.

And so that is how Kate got a designer wedding gown marked down from $2,200 to $1,200 and marked down again to $900.

Next, Kate and Joe had to find someone to officiate at their wedding. They had already gotten their marriage certificate at City Hall, but they needed someone to do the ceremony.

"I have a friend who does weddings," said Brenda.

"But the wedding's on Sunday. He's probably booked up already."

"The good news is that he's a rabbi, so he's probably available on a Sunday. He's actually a playwright. He only does marriages on the side, at Riker's Island."

"The correctional institution?"

"Yes."

"Okay," said Kate. "Give him a call and if he's available, I'm sure Joe will be fine with it. He grew up Catholic and Protestant on both sides and I'm Jewish. But we agreed that a rabbi doing the ceremony will be acceptable."

Brenda called Rabbi Abraham and he said "yes," on the condition that the couple agreed to his $250 fee, and that he could meet them in advance.

He also had a second condition to be met before he'd consent to officiate the wedding on such short notice. It was a requirement that Brenda didn't share with her best friend. He told Brenda she had to promise to go back to AA after she confided in him that she was drinking again. "Okay, Rabbi," said Brenda. "What meeting do you go to? Is it virtual or in-person?" After he gave Brenda the details, she ended the phone call and shared with Kate that they had someone to officiate the wedding.

Two hours later, Kate and Joe found themselves entering the four-floor walk-up apartment to Rabbi Abraham's residence on the upper west side.

"Come in," Rabbi Abraham said. "Have a seat."

There were boxes everywhere. Kate was having a hard time finding a place to sit.

"You just moved in?" she asked.

"Yes. A year ago."

Finally, Joe pushed books and other items off of some of the boxes. He pushed down on the boxes and determined there were two that were sturdy enough to support Kate. He could stand.

"Let's get started," said Rabbi Abraham.

"Thanks for doing this on such short notice," said Joe.

"I'm happy to help out. Brenda and I go way back. We were in a support group together. It's confidential so I can't tell you which one."

"No need to go into details," said Kate who guessed what he was referring to.

"None of my business," said Joe.

"So now for the sixty-four-thousand-dollar question."

"Go ahead. Ask us anything."

"Why do you want to get married? Kate? You first"

"Because I want to start a family."

"But why don't you just live together?" Rabbi Abraham asked.

"I'm not opposed to cohabitating," Kate continued. "That's fine for many. But for me, I like the legality of marriage. I like that it *is* permanent. Okay, so if it doesn't work out, you can get divorced. But at least you start off saying, and acting, like it will be forever.

Kate took a deep breath and continued, "But starting a family isn't the only reason I want to marry Joe. I love him. Yes, I love Joe with all my heart. I've only known him a few weeks, but he is the smartest, kindest, most handsome, loving, and considerate man I've met…ever. Most of all, Joe 'gets' me."

"Okay, whatever 'gets' me means!" said Rabbi Abraham. "So, young man," the rabbi continued, turning to Joe. "Why do *you* want to get married?"

"I love Kate. Kate loves me. We want to spend our lives together. We want to have a family together. It's as simple as that."

"Great. So, I'll see you both on Sunday."

"Yes."

"Did you bring the money?"

"I have the money, but I thought we'd give it to you on Sunday."

"I've been doing this a long time," Rabbi Abraham said. "I can't count how many times I do this pre-marriage interview and how many times one of the two back out before the big event. So now I am asking for the fee in advance. That's right. It's a non-refundable fee. I'm reserving that time for you so if either of you back out before Sunday, that's on you. I still get paid."

"We're not backing out."

With that, Kate stood up from the box she was sitting on. Joe gave the rabbi his fee, and then took Kate's hand, escorting her out the door of the rabbi's cluttered apartment. As they left, the door knob came off and clattered onto the floor.

"Oh, don't worry about that," the rabbi shouted out. "It happens all the time. I'll reattach it."

Chapter 12

Joe was back in Kate's apartment. Fortunately, she had a Queen-sized bed since they agreed it made sense for Joe initially to move in with Kate. Kate had another six months on her lease and over the next month or two, they could discuss if they wanted to renew Kate's lease or find another apartment elsewhere. Or they could ask to be put on the waiting list for a two-bedroom since Kate only had a one-bedroom, one-bath apartment. It was a long waiting list since the two bedrooms in her building were unique in that every two bedroom also had two bathrooms.

Until then, they agreed Joe would put a desk in the corner of the living room to use when he needed to write. Kate would continue going to the shared office space she was renting, at least till her one-year commitment expired in four more months. They could reevaluate their situation at that time since they both agreed, as an older couple used to living on their own, having their own space was fundamental for their marriage to work.

Without warning, Kate felt the need to throw up. She rushed to the bathroom where she puked in the toilet.

"Glad I made it in time," Kate said as she wiped her mouth clean with a paper towel.

"What was that from?" asked Joe.

"Must be something I ate. It could have been the brunch at the Plaza or your mother's cooking. Sorry I said that. Your mother's cooking was great."

"I ate everything you ate and I'm okay," said Joe.

"That's not true. I ate a few different dishes than you," Kate replied.

"Okay. But still, it's been two days. Food poisoning usually happens within the first twelve hours of ingesting the contaminated food," Joe continued.

"What else could it be?" Kate asked.

***

Joe sat in the waiting room of the OB/GYN that a friend of Kate's had recommended. She could have asked Melanie, but Kate didn't want to say anything until she was sure.

A nurse dressed in blue scrubs came out of the back area of the office and said to Joe, "You can go in now."

In the small examination room, Kate lay on an exam table. A white cloth covered her up.

There was a television monitor next to her. Doctor Johnson, a Black woman who looked like she was in her mid-thirties, smeared gel on Kate's abdomen. She then moved the ultrasound device used to do fetal monitoring.

Kate looked at the monitor and then she looked back at Joe, who was also staring at the monitor, in disbelief.

"Is that what I think it is?" Joe asked the doctor.

"I see a gestational sac," the doctor replied.

"What does that mean?" asked Kate.

"You people are having a baby," Doctor Johnson replied.

Kate held Joe's hand tightly, squeezing it so hard when they heard those words from the doctor that he was afraid she might have broken one of his fingers.

"How does it look? I mean do you think everything is okay?" Joe asked.

"The embryo isn't visible yet, " said the doctor. "But everything seems fine for five weeks."

Joe's expression changed from awe, to shock.

"Five weeks?"

Joe glanced at Kate, who was beaming.

"Congratulations," Doctor Johnson continued, wiping the excess gel with a tissue. "I've got to run, but my Nurse can answer your questions. Be sure you make a follow-up appointment for next week, after the holidays. We'll do another ultrasound. We should be able to see more. Because of your age, we want to monitor you closely, young woman."

With that, the doctor bustled out of the room, pausing only long enough to peel off her gloves and drop them, and the tissue, into a trash receptacle. Joe had many unanswered questions. He tried to wait, to think things through, since Kate seemed absolutely thrilled with the news.

But by the time they reached her apartment and let themselves inside, Joe just had to ask.

"Kate," he said. "The doctor said five weeks."

"I know. So, we won't tell anyone till the end of my first trimester. They say that's when most miscarriages happen. So, in another seven weeks we can tell everyone. It's going to be hard to keep this secret from Brenda. How about we tell Brenda and Dennis at the same time, but we swear them to secrecy?" Kate asked.

There was a long pause before Joe added, "When do you think it happened?"

"I think we had beginner's luck, as they say," Kate replied, with a big smile on her face. She puttered around the kitchen, putting on the kettle for tea.

"But you and I have only known each other for three weeks."

Kate's smile disappeared. She turned to face him.

"What are you saying, Joe?"

"Five weeks means it probably isn't mine."

There was a silence between them that went on for a minute or two, but it seemed much longer. It was only interrupted by a siren blaring outside which they could hear from the window of Kate's apartment.

"I don't know what to say," Kate said, breaking through the silence.

Joe was still stunned. He strode to the table where he had placed his laptop and shoved it into his backpack.

Without another word, Joe headed for the door.

"Where are you going?" Kate asked.

"I can't stay," Joe replied.

"Why not? I thought we were getting married?"

"We were getting married, in just three days, but I don't think I can marry you if you're carrying some other man's child."

"What do you mean 'some other man's child'? If it's not yours, then it's got to be Jennings's. I don't sleep around!"

"I didn't mean to imply that," Joe said, sadly. "I know that it would be Jennings's. Your former flame. I don't think this is the way to enter our exclusive union together, or to start our own family."

Kate started sobbing.

"I'm sorry I'm making you cry. My heart is broken, too."

With that, Joe left Kate's apartment.

Joe, with nowhere else to go, headed back to Dennis's flat. He was reluctant to tell Dennis what happened because he feared his best friend would tell him a version of "I told you so."

Kate, meanwhile, went straight to Brenda's. She needed support. Joe was gone and Kate knew she faced a rough road ahead. But at thirty-nine, even if she had to go it alone, there was no question on her mind that she was going to keep her baby.

"You have to tell Jennings," Brenda said, after giving her best friend a long hug. "This is great news. I'm sure he'll see it that way."

"I'm not as confident as you, but I know I have to tell him."

An hour later, Kate entered the health club where Jennings had a membership. It was practically his second home after his penthouse apartment. Kate found him on the squash court. It was hard for her to stay angry at Jennings since she was still so attracted to him. In addition to his debonair charm, he was exceptionally handsome man with fiery red hair that contrasted with the light, neutral tones of his squash apparel.

"What are you doing here?" Jennings asked.

"I have something to tell you."

"You already told me you're getting married. Is the wedding off?"

"Yes."

"But you know I still need more time," Jennings replied.

"It's not that. Can we go somewhere to talk?"

"There's a café area on the main floor. Meet me there in five minutes. Let me finish up this match," Jennings said.

Five minutes later, still in his squash outfit, holding his racquet, Jennings showed up at the café.

"Let's get two coffees and sit down and talk," Jennings said. "I have fifteen minutes before my next match."

"No coffee for me," Kate said.

"That's a first. I've never seen you turn down coffee." He glanced at her purse, opened, on the table. "Don't see your cigarettes, either."

"I have a good reason," Kate began. She gulped and then she spit it out. "Jennings, I'm pregnant."

"Well congratulations! I know how much you wanted to start a family. You and that new boyfriend of yours should be thrilled."

"That's just it. The doctor said the fetus is a perfect size for five weeks."

"Wow! They can tell you're pregnant soon these days! Good for you again."

"Jennings, you're not hearing me. I only have known Joe, his name is Joe, for three weeks."

"So, what are you saying?"

"That the baby isn't his."

Jennings sat very still. "So are you saying…"

"Yes."

"Oh no," Jennings responded.

There was another silence. After a few moments, Jennings cleared his throat and said, "The good news is that it's early enough that you can still have an abortion."

Kate couldn't stop herself from slapping Jennings across the face. It was a violent act she immediately regretted.

"Sorry, Jennings. That was uncalled for."

"No, you're right. That was insensitive of me. Okay, here's another suggestion."

"Yes?"

"How about we get married?" Jennings blurted out.

"What are you talking about?"

"Well, you were getting married anyway. He broke it off, right? Isn't that why you're here? Why not me instead of that other guy?"

"Joe. His name was…I mean is…Joe."

"Yes, Joe. Let's you and me do the right thing and get married."

"But you said you needed more time."

"But this kid needs a father and a good name. *My* good name."

Kate started to smile, but it was a forced smile.

"Okay. Why not? We already have the rabbi…"

"Rabbi?"

"Yes, the rabbi for Riker's Island prison was going to officiate."

"Okay, unless I can come up with someone else."

"I'll agree to that."

"Any other details we have to take care of?"

"We ordered some food and champagne to be delivered that day. Nothing fancy but something the guests could munch on. Chocolate covered strawberries. An assortment of cheeses, A vegetable crudité. Crackers. But we definitely need a venue. We were going to get married in Joe's best friend's apartment. That can't happen now."

"We'll have it at my place. There's plenty of room."

"Okay! Thanks."

"So, it's settled. Now I'd like to get back to my next squash game."

"But—"

"It's with one of my most important wealth management clients. I must decide what my strategy will be. He's not a very good player. Do I let him win because that might help our working relationship or do I give it my all and win no matter what because I'm the better player?"

"I'm sure you'll figure it out," Kate said.

With that, he grabbed his racket and headed back to the game. She watched Jennings go, still in shock about everything happening so fast.

***

Later that night, as Kate rested in her apartment, she was trying to figure out what she'd do about the upcoming Spring semester classes. *I can still teach,* she told herself since she wouldn't really show till April or May, toward the end of the semester. She wouldn't even tell the department chair she was pregnant until she was showing. She didn't want them to give away the classes she still hoped to teach in the fall to another professor. As an assistant professor, even though tenure was not a possibility for five or more years down the road, Kate was still aware how fortunate she was to have landed a fulltime position so soon after receiving her doctorate. The full-time status gave her certain rights that she would not have as a part-time or adjunct professor. Maybe Kate would just take off one semester in the Fall for maternity leave, returning to the college to teach the following Spring. She had to check her contract. Legally they might have to keep her full-time position open for her.

Joe and Dennis were hanging out at another single's bar near his apartment. They were each on their third beer. Joe didn't have to drive, but he did want to avoid getting drunk.

"I can't believe this is happening, Dennis," Joe said.

"It's good you found out before the wedding," said Dennis. "Who wants to raise some other guy's kid?"

As Dennis said that, Joe thought to himself, *I'd do it. I want Kate.*

"Of course, you're right about that," Joe said, placating his friend. Joe was reluctant to share how he really felt. That he was getting used to the baby idea and maybe didn't care who the father was.

After another hour of commiserating, Joe told Dennis he wanted to go.

"Okay," Dennis said. "I have a couple of errands to run. I'll see you back at the apartment."

Joe went off on his own, walking down street after street. The brisk air, in the high 40s, felt good. After a few blocks, as if he was wandering in a fog, Joe found himself outside the doctor's office he and Kate had gone to the day before.

Doctor Johnson, the gynecologist that gave Kate the ultrasound, was exiting the building at the same time.

"Hi," said Joe.

"Hello," Doctor Johnson replied.

"I don't know if you remember me. I'm the man from that couple yesterday that you said it was the perfect size for a five-week fetus."

"I remember. Congratulations again."

"No, you don't understand. You shattered my world."

"Why? You don't want to become a father?" asked Doctor Johnson.

"It's not that. I only met Kate three weeks ago. So, if it's a five-week fetus, it can't be mine."

Doctor Johnson stopped in her tracks. She looked Joe straight in the eyes and she said, "I didn't say a five-week fetus. I said, 'It's perfect for five weeks,' or words to that effect."

"I don't see the difference."

"I was referring to what we physicians call the LMP or last menstrual period, which is two weeks *before* conception.

"So when would conception have occurred?"

"I can confidently say it occurred three weeks ago. The five weeks is the gestational age of the fetus."

Joe couldn't help himself. He gave Doctor Johnson a big kiss on her cheek and a powerful hug.

"Doctor Johnson. I love you. What I mean is that I love what you just told me. So, I *could* be the father!"

"Well, if you're the only man your girlfriend had sex with three weeks ago, then you are the father. And if you have any questions, somewhere between seven and nine weeks into your girlfriend's pregnancy, you can take a prenatal paternity test to definitively confirm who the father is."

"That won't be necessary, Doctor Johnson, but it's nice to know that option exists. But there's one more thing, Doctor Johnson."

"What's that?"

"I used a condom," said Joe.

"Condoms are only ninety-eight percent effective," explained Doctor Johnson.

There was a pause before Joe replied, "It must be that two percent that gets some couples every time."

"I understand finding out you're probably the father, especially since you used a condom, must be a shock."

"You don't understand, doctor," replied Joe. "From what you've said, now that I know I could be the father, I realize I know it even more in my heart."

"That's good to hear," responded Doctor Johnson, "because even though biology is important, love and nurturing is even more important."

"You're right about that. In fact, I was a fool to let paternity influence my actions."

"I wouldn't call you a fool, but I do know, from my professional experience, that the baby doesn't care who the father is, or who's loving it, or feeding it. All the baby cares about is that it has somebody to love. Another thing. Fathering a baby is easy. Almost any man can do that. But being a father. That's something else. That's a rare privilege. Do you love her?"

"Yes."

"Whatta ya doing here, then?"

Joe got a panicked look on his face.

"You're so right! Sorry, Doc, I have to run. I have to fix things, if I can. I've made a mess of everything."

Joe rushed off toward Kate's apartment. He was so happy and overwrought by what he just learned that he wasn't paying attention as he stepped out into Third Avenue while punching in Kate's number on his cell phone.

A truck veered out of nowhere. Sounds of honking and skidding tires shattered the silence.

Joe stopped.

Looked up.

Dropped his phone.

Thwack!

It took five minutes for the ambulance to get there, which wasn't that long considering it was Christmas time and Manhattan.

The paramedics loaded Joe into the ambulance. Within moments he was on his way to the nearest hospital for urgent care.

Dennis was listed as Joe's local next of kin, with his parents after that. As first name on the contact list, Dennis got there in just thirty minutes.

"How's he doing?" Dennis asked the attending physician.

“He’s in the ICU. He’s stable, but pretty well banged-up. We have to do an MRI and see if there was any brain damage. It’s a good thing it’s Christmas time and that truck was driving no more than five or ten miles an hour. Your brother…”

“My best friend,” Dennis said, correcting the doctor.

“Your friend got hit, but he’s lucky to be alive and even luckier that he may have escaped life threatening internal damage.”

“What’s the next step?”

“We will keep him overnight or longer, depending on the MRI results.”

“Sounds like a plan.”

Fortunately, the MRI showed no permanent damage. Joe’s pain medication, though, was strong, and he slept in his hospital room for the next twelve hours.

Dennis stayed by his side. He was surprised that Kate didn’t show up at the hospital, but considering how things ended between she and Joe, he understood why she’d stay away. She sent her friend Brenda in her place.

Thanks to Brenda, Dennis learned that Kate was marrying Jennings the next day. Since Joe's accident happened before he had a chance to tell Dennis or Kate the good news, that the baby was his, Dennis figured it was for the best that Kate was marrying Jennings.

December 29th. Joe finally opened his eyes.

"Where am I?"

"You're at Bellevue Hospital," Dennis replied.

"Oh," Joe moaned. "I feel like I got hit by a truck."

"You did! You got hit by a truck."

"Is that a joke?"

"No. That's what happened."

"What day is it?"

"I'm supposed to ask you that question. That's how we know if there's any brain damage."

"No, Dennis, you need to tell me what day it is."

"It's December 29th."

"Kate and I were supposed to get married on December 29,th" Joe replied

"I know."

"I feel like an idiot," said Joe.

"Why? Because you didn't want to marry a woman who's carrying another man's child?"

"That it shouldn't have mattered if I really loved Kate. And I ran into the doctor who gave Kate the ultrasound and it turned out, she mis-spoke. When she said, 'perfect for five weeks' she meant five weeks as a gestational age, from Kate's last menstrual period."

"Which means?"

"She said she should have told us that the baby was perfect for a *three-week* fetus."

"I get it now!" Dennis said, like a light bulb went off in his head.

"Yes. In fact, I was trying to call Kate to tell her what the doctor said when I crossed at Third Avenue."

"That's where it happened. You've been in here ever since."

"I have to tell Kate."

"It's probably too late," Dennis said. "Brenda told me she's marrying Jennings today in his penthouse. She told me something about her and Kate went there recently to bring him chicken soup?"

"Yeah, I heard all about that. but, what? They're getting married *today*! I can't let that happen!"

"But the doctor wants to look you over again when he does his rounds," said Dennis.

"F—that! Look. Just get me in that wheelchair. Let's get out of this place."

"I don't want to be arrested for trying to leave the hospital without paying your bill."

"Don't worry about it. I'm sure they found the insurance information in my wallet. They'll be fine. But Kate and me. We won't be fine if I don't get out of here."

"Okay. I'll be your partner in crime."

"They always take a patient out to the parking lot in a wheelchair so no one will suspect anything."

"What do I say if someone stops us?"

"Discharged. That's the word you want to use, *discharged*."

"Where are your clothes?"

Joe looked around. Then pointed.

"Looks like everything's in those oversized plastic bags on the window ledge over there. Shoes and all."

"Okay, my friend, let's go," said Dennis.

Like a scene out of a movie, Dennis pushed Joe through the hospital corridors, into the elevator, and out the front entrance. Fortunately, a taxi was letting a fare out just as Dennis was wheeling his friend to that exact spot.

"Are you available?" Dennis asked the driver.

"Yes."

"Okay. Thanks. We're going to midtown. Just give me a few minutes to get my friend into the cab."

"Do you need any assistance?"

"We're in a rush and I can handle it."

With that, Dennis scooped Joe out of the wheelchair, pushing him on to the back seat.

"Can I sit in the front?" Dennis asked. "My friend is stretched out in the back so it will be hard for me to sit."

"Sure. Hop up here."

With that, they sped off toward Seventh Avenue and 52nd Street, where Jennings had his spacious penthouse apartment. Traffic was heavy but that was to be expected Christmas week in New York City. So many tourists would be arriving so they could at least once go to Times Square on New Year's Eve to see the ball drop.

Dennis put the $40 cab ride, including tip, on his credit card.

"May I help you?" said the doorman who greeted their taxi and opened the cab door.

"I'd much appreciate it," Dennis replied. "We're here for a wedding."

The doorman frowned, eyeing their less than formal attire. "The Jennings/Hellman wedding?"

"That's the one."

The doorman straightened. "You've got a few minutes to freshen-up. I understand the invitation called for two o'clock and it's just one-thirty now."

Chapter 13

It was hard for Joe to walk but he leaned on Dennis and made it inside the swank apartment building and to the front desk.

"What's your name, sir?" the concierge at the front desk asked. His name tag said "Vinny."

"Hi, there, Vinny. This is my friend Dennis, and I'm Joe Wexler."

"I have a list of guests for the wedding here. I don't see either name on that list."

"I'm a last-minute addition," Joe said.

"Wait. I see a note from the bride at the bottom of the list: 'Do not grant entry to someone by the name of Joe Wexler.' Didn't you say your name is Joe Wexler?"

"Did I say that?" asked Joe.

"Yes, you did. Then I must ask you to leave or I'll have to call security."

"I'm not leaving! I've got to stop that wedding!"

Vinny picked up the desk phone. "I'm calling the police now," he said.

"Why? Are you going to have me arrested for being in love?"

The concierge put down the phone.

"What do you mean?" asked Vinny.

"Look, we don't have much time. Let me explain this as succinctly as possible. The bride and I fell in love. Then we found out she was pregnant. The doctor made a mistake, and we were led to believe the new baby was fathered by the guy she's marrying now. But it turns out, it probably *is* my baby after all, so I want to —I must —stop their wedding so I can marry the bride instead."

There was a pause.

"Look, Vinny, I realize I was being a jerk. I have to apologize to the bride so she can decide if she still wants to marry Jennings. If she does, I'll give them my blessing. But right now, I've got to get up there and apologize. The bride upstairs is about to make a big mistake, and she doesn't even know it."

"Okay. I'll let you up there," said Vinny.

"What's that?" asked Joe.

Finally, with the debate behind them, Dennis and Joe made their way as quickly as possible considering Joe's condition to the penthouse elevator.

The penthouse door was open. At least fifty people stood in Jennings's expansive living room area. Joe could see there were original paintings by Andy Warhol, David Hockney, and Lee Krasner, Jackson Pollock's widow and a renowned artist in her own right. There were also antique armchairs and cabinets throughout the room. The oversized windows let in the beautiful midday light. You could even see Central Park from one of the windows.

"Where's the bride?" Joe asked the bartender.

"She's old-fashioned, so I've been told she's still in the bedroom. She didn't want anyone to see her before the wedding, not even the groom."

Joe turned to Dennis. "You coming with me?" But Dennis had planted himself beside the makeshift open bar. "No, you go on ahead and do your declaration and your apology and begging for forgiveness thing on your own. I'll be out here."

Joe turned and hobbled through a hallway to the first bedroom. He opened the door. No Kate.

How many bedrooms are there in this penthouse, Joe said to himself.

He opened bedroom door number two. Still no Kate.

Then he opened bedroom door, number three. That must have been the primary because it was twice as big as the other two bedrooms.

"There you are!" Joe said.

"What are you doing here?" Kate demanded. "Get out, now!" She looked at him more closely. "What happened? You look like you've been hit by a truck."

"Please. I have something important to tell you."

"What could you have to tell me that I possibly want to hear?"

"I realized I was a jerk, yes, a jerk. I don't care whose baby it is, Kate. I love you and I want to marry you and start a family together."

"You think you can just barge in here and expect me to take you back?" asked Kate.

"I just don't want you to make the biggest mistake of your life by marrying Jennings. I hope you can find it in your heart to still love me even though I've been a jerk."

“I’m glad you used the word ‘*jerk*’ although that’s a much kinder word than I would have used.”

“Kate. It didn’t hit me until it was too late. Falling in love, Kate. These days, that’s as much a miracle as giving birth. I love you, Kate. And I don’t know if I’m ever gonna feel this way toward anyone else. I just need you to know that if you still feel you have to go through marrying Jennings.”

Kate turned around. Her eyes were filled with tears.

“There’s something else I have to tell you.”

Joe repeated what he found out from the doctor in as condensed a way as possible. Upon hearing the news, Kate began to cry even louder.

“Why are you crying?”

“I’m crying because that’s such a relief.”

“I agree. So, we can get married now?”

“Not so fast,” Kate said. “I’m furious that you weren’t going to marry me when you thought Jennings was the father of my unborn child.”

“You mean ‘our unborn child.’”

“Well, you obviously didn’t see it that way,” said Kate.

"That's true. I've apologized. I told you I know I've been a jerk. I'm so sorry, Kate. But I love you and I want to marry you and start—well, we've already started—a family together. Okay, so I've let you down. I let you down big time. But that's what happens with couples from time to time."

Kate grabbed a tissue from the nightstand and whiped the mascara that was underneath her eyes from crying.

"I know Jennings was only marrying me because he felt he had to 'do the right thing,'" Kate sobbed.

"So, you're saying 'yes'?"

"I would like to make you suffer a little while longer. You deserve to suffer the way you made me suffer, but we have guests in the living room waiting for a wedding."

"At least fifty. Maybe even more by now!"

"It's not fair to them," said Kate.

Most of the guests were from Jennings's side: his squash buddies, business associates, several neighbors, and various friends. Kate's parents drove back from Philadelphia and so did Kate's sister Melanie and Jerry. Several professors in Kate's department were in attendance as well. They were available since it was already winter break from teaching.

"Can you call Jennings? Ask him to come in here?"

"Sure."

Kate retrieved her cell phone from the white satin bag from a vintage clothing shop that was a gift from her other best friend, Serena, who drove all the way from State College, Pennsylvania to attend Kate's wedding. Serena knew it would be hard for her to be far from her cell phone, even on her wedding day, so she got her bag large enough to accommodate her phone. Kate texted Jennings quickly, and then she looked at Joe.

"I told him to come into the bedroom. I told him it's an emergency."

Several minutes later, Jennings appeared. He was wearing a dark suit. He had a red handkerchief tucked in his top pocket. He looked dapper and younger than his forty-eight years.

"What's up, Kate? We're about to start the ceremony."

Jennings suddenly noticed someone else was in the room with them.

"Who's this?" asked Jennings.

"Jennings, this is Joe. Joe, this is Jennings."

"What's *he* doing here? He looks like he's been hit by a—"

"We know!" Kate and Joe said at the same time.

Kate rushed her words. "Jennings, it turns out the doctor made a mistake and the baby is Joe's."

"I'm glad we got that straightened out. I have to process what you just told me, Kate. But I also don't want to embarrass myself. Almost all the people in that living room are my friends or my business associates or clients. They were told I was getting married today. They don't even know about the baby part."

"Wait a minute. You'd marry me now, so you won't lose face?" Kate asked, exasperated.

"We can wait a short while and get a divorce. Irreconcilable differences, etcetera, etcetera," Jennings added.

"I can't believe you're more concerned with embarrassing yourself in front of your guests than feeling at least some sadness that the baby isn't yours."

"You're not being very grateful, Kate. I told you I needed more time, but you pushed and pushed. And now that I'm giving you what you want, a wedding, you're telling me that you'd rather marry this guy instead just because it turns out he's the father of your baby."

"No! I want to marry this guy instead because he's in love with me and he wants to spend his life with me. And I'm in love with him!"

"Okay, okay. I see your point. Look, since everyone's here, including the rabbi, and since we were going to have a wedding anyway, let's just switch out who the groom is. I'll make an announcement and any guests who want to leave can leave, but we might as well have the wedding go forward."

"That's pretty magnanimous of you," Joe said.

"And you get to stay single," Kate added.

"True," Jennings agreed.

Only a dozen of the guests chose to leave after Jennings announced that the bride was marrying Joe Wexler instead. The remaining guests from Jennings's side were enjoying the refreshments and beverages and the ambiance.

"I'm confused," said the rabbi. "Which one of you is the groom?"

"I am," said Joe.

"That's great. I remember you and I met recently with the bride," said Rabbi Abraham.

"Yes, that's right."

"Let's get on with the ceremony." *And I thought prison weddings were complicated,*" the rabbi muttered to himself.

Outside Jennings's apartment building, Joe limped along with Kate holding him up as the well-wishers threw rice at them. It was said that the custom began with the ancient Romans and Celts as it symbolized fertility and prosperity. But Kate and Joe did not need the fertility part of the custom.

Kate turned her back on the crowd as she flung her bouquet in the air. Brenda, with tears in her eyes, caught the bouquet.

As a taxi whisked Kate and Joe away, Dennis approached Brenda, still holding the bouquet.

"Hey. You wanta get a drink?"

Brenda wiped her nose, dotted her teary eyes with a tissue, and smiled at Dennis.

"I'd love to. But can we make it a coffee?"

As the crowd moved away from the building's entrance, a somewhat confused Vinny the concierge asked Jennings, "How was the wedding?"

"It was perfect, Vinny. Just perfect."

Vinny scratched his head. "As long as everything worked out to your satisfaction, Mr. Jennings."

"Vinny, I did a good deed today, my friend. All in the name of true love."

"I heard about what happened, sir," said Vinny. "You did a good deed today, indeed."

"Yes," Jennings grinned. "And now, it's party time!"

"Where to?" the taxi driver asked.

"Joe, should we go to my apartment?"

"I think we should make a quick stop at the hospital first. I left in a hurry and need to get officially checked out."

"Sounds good. While you're doing that, I have some business to take care of."

"I know you're on semester break. Is it a time management client? Someone who's been a victim who needs you to advocate for them? If it's business, that can't wait?"

"Neither of those situations. Actually, there are several dates for next week that I forgot to cancel when we first decided to get married."

"Really? How many dates are we talking about?"

"Just six or so."

"Six!" Joe responded.

"I told you I was a woman on a mission. And I hate to waste them. Maybe I should ask Brenda to fill in for me…"

Chapter 14

Ten months later.

A robot wife with a flowery dress covering most of the robot entered Kate and Joe's bedroom. The room was large enough to accommodate the baby's bassinet, the robot wife, and their two visitors. Their new two-bedroom apartment was perfect for their growing family.

"Is it time for me to rock the bassinet?" the robot wife asked in a distinctly robotic voice.

"No, thank you," said Joe. "We're in here now. We have visitors. Can you finish doing the dishes and then can you vacuum the living room rug?"

"Yes, Mr. Wexler," the robot wife said in her machinelike voice.

"Joe, when is the robot husband prototype going to be ready? I've had a lot of customer requests for it," said Dennis.

"I'm working on it, partner. You'll be the first to know."

“Oh, yeah? And who’s the model for the robot husband prototype?”

“Why, Jennings, of course,” Kate answered, with a smile.

Dennis nodded. “I know you’ve been busy with Kate and the baby, Joe, but we can’t let our business slide.”

“Or on finishing your novel, dear” added Kate.

“Yes, I’ll get to it all. But this little guy. He’s my priority and Kate knows all about prioritizing.”

“I love the name you gave your son. Oliver. I looked it up. It stands for ‘olive tree planter,’” said Brenda. “Olive trees are notable for their longevity.”

“Yes,” said Kate. “Some have been known to live over two thousand years.”

They all gazed at Oliver in his bassinet. He was an adorable infant, all smiles.

“We’re soon moving Oliver into his crib in the first bedroom. He’s getting too big for the bassinet. It’s going to be tough for him to be separated from us, but it’s time.

“That happens around three months,” said Joe.

“It’s going to be tough for Oliver to be separated from you both or the other way around?” asked Brenda.

“You’re so right,” said Joe. “I never knew I could get that attached to someone in the way I’ve gotten attached to Kate and now to Oliver.”

“Look at this little guy,” said Dennis.

“Babies are so cute,” said Brenda.

“Does it make you want to start your own family?” Kate said, as she stared directly at Dennis and then at Brenda.

“No comment,” said Brenda.

“Ditto,” said Dennis.

“He has my eyes,” said Kate as she returned her attention to Oliver.

“That’s my chin,” said Joe, the doting father.

“He definitely has your smile, Kate” said Brenda.

Kate looked at Joe, then at Oliver, and felt something she had always recommended in her time-management seminars but had never truly achieved for herself: total, uninterrupted presence.

For the first time ever, she wasn't counting minutes, milestones, or worrying about missed chances—everything that mattered had arrived exactly when, and even how, it was supposed to.

##

About the Author

Jan Yager is a prolific author of fiction, nonfiction, dramatic literature, screenplays, and poetry. *Just in Time for Love* is her fifth novel. She also has a Ph.D. in sociology and is an Adjunct Associate Professor teaching sociology, criminology, and victimology courses at several colleges and universities. Time management is another area of expertise for Jan.

Happily married to Fred Yager for more than four decades, they have raised two sons, Scott and Jeff, who now have families of their own.

About the Screenwriter

Fred Yager co-wrote "No Time for Love," with Jan Yager, the screenplay upon which the novella *Just in Time for Love* is based. Fred studied filmmaking at NYU. He was also the film critic and entertainment writer for the Associated Press for four years. His screenplays "Getting Connected" and "Proud Mary" were optioned by director Walter Hill and producer Aaron Russo, respectively.

In addition to publishing seven novels including *Botanica,* co-authored with Jeff Yager, and *The Asian Queen,* and *Cybersona,* Fred has held corporate editing, writing, and producing jobs.

Other novels by Jan Yager

Untimely Death

Available in e-book, print, and audiobook formats.

When a sudden death shatters the lives of those left behind, secrets surface that refuse to stay buried. This gripping novel explores how one untimely death ripples through families, friendships, and investigations—revealing that the truth is often far more dangerous than the crime itself. Dr. Kimberly Stone, a criminology professor, is forced to become an amateur sleuth to solve her best friend and colleague's murder before she's the next victim.

"*Untimely Death* reads like the work of a master of the detective thriller...." —*Independent Publisher*

"The Yagers have written a winner"—*Associated Press*

"A fascinating piece of work."—Andrew M. Greeley, bestselling author of *Wages of Sin*

Completed spec screenplay is available.

Just Your Everyday People

Available in e-book, print, and audiobook versions.

Behind ordinary lives and familiar faces lurk hidden motives and quiet betrayals. This unsettling psychological suspense novel proves that "everyday people" are capable of extraordinary—and sometimes chilling—choices.

"The friendship between two married couples begins to unravel when one of the wives seduces a stranger in a bar. Blackmail, betrayal and murder ensue[…]"—*Publishers Weekly*

"*Just Your Everyday People* isn't your everyday read. It's a sneaky little thriller that explores the underside of suburban life […]" —John Lutz, best-selling novelist, *Single White Female*

Completed spec screenplay is available.

On the Run

Available in e-book, print, and audiobook formats.

Two 17-year-olds from opposite sides of the tracks cross paths while running from the lives they can no longer bear. As their journey unfolds, the connection they form changes them in ways neither could have imagined—proving that sometimes escape leads not away from life, but straight into it.

Based on a screenplay, "On the Run," by Fred Yager and Jan Yager.

Completed spec screenplay is available.

The Pretty One

Available in e-book, print, and audiobook formats.

Beauty can open doors—but it can also trap you behind expectations you never chose. This compelling novel explores identity, rivalry, and self-worth, revealing the hidden costs of being "the pretty one."

Dr. Emily Taylor seems to have it all-she's thin, attractive, happily married with children, and has a successful therapy practice and writing career-when she is interviewed on a major talk show to discuss her bestseller. When success catapults Emily on a food binge and her weight climbs over 200, Emily realizes she has to deal with the underlying causes to the compulsive overeating that she battles.

"A fine and uplifting read, with many perspectives, highly recommended." — *Midwest Book Review*

www.ingramcontent.com/pod-product-compliance
Lightning Source LLC
Chambersburg PA
CBHW011521240626
47154CB00009B/2922

* 9 7 8 1 9 3 8 9 9 8 1 8 8 *